SPECIAL EDITION

PRISONER 120518

SPECIAL EDITION

PRISONER 120518

RED RAIN #2.5

**RACHEL NEWHOUSE
& DAVID HARTUNG**

rachelnewhouse.com

MAY 2076

MAY 2076

1

Rott was an island, and that was really all that could be said about it.

Like most prisons, it was a tasteless mass of concrete. The guard towers and cramped barracks had long since crowded out most of the sand from the shore, their barnacle-crusted foundations disappearing into the water with high tide. There was no need for a barbed wire fence—the open waters of the frigid North Atlantic had the same effect. Cold wind whipped mercilessly across the yard at all hours, and the only thing that disrupted the monotony was the occasional silhouette of a passing ship.

I had been shuffled between five prisons in so many months, but this reassignment had a finality about it. Maybe it was the location—a dead-end in the middle of the ocean—maybe it was the name. I'd like to think the name was a sadistic pun, but the United had literally never done anything clever during its illustrious tyranny, so I assumed the name was just a happy accident.

Still, the island definitely seemed like a place where you left things to decompose. I was confident that's what the government intended to do with me.

They assigned me the number 120518 because it was convenient; the patch for the jumpsuit had just been sent up from the morgue, and the secretary hadn't put it away yet.

I immediately donned a nickname, because I was told that's what all the prisoners did. I chose Quetzalcoatl. The name had no significance, except that it was as far removed from my real name as possible, and I enjoyed watching the secretary suffer when she tried to spell it.

It didn't matter what they called me. Personally, I had zero intentions of learning anybody's name, real or assumed, on this island. Anytime someone was so rude as to introduce themselves, I made a concentrated effort to purge their name from my mind as soon as they walked away. I didn't want to know anyone, and I didn't want anyone to know me. I wasn't here to make friends.

The only person whose name I retained was Tower. He was a guard. You can guess where he was stationed.

I'd asked him for the time once while taking a lap around the yard, and he had the audacity to introduce himself. Since he was one of the few reliable sources of time, I decided to let it slide.

I took laps because I had nothing better to do. There was plenty of activity on the island; most of the prisoners had been assigned to a nearly-complete construction project in the middle of the yard. Based on the random bits of machinery that were continually getting delivered, I assumed it was a factory, but I hadn't bothered to ask. I hadn't been assigned to work on it; in fact, I hadn't been assigned a job at all.

I wasn't sure if my unemployment was error or slight, but I was in no rush to correct their mistake. I figured if I took laps and acted like I had somewhere to be, no one would pay me any mind. So far, it was working.

My incarceration went swimmingly until my 29th day on Rott. That's when everything went to hell. Never mind it was a short trip.

It was a bright, but not in any way cheery, day, and I was getting another lap in before dinner. I had just passed under Tower's station when I heard the shout.

"42."

I jumped, mainly because this was the first time he had initiated a conversation. I glanced up at the control booth that sat atop the three-story tower. The window was open, and I could see him sitting there, but he wasn't looking at me. His eyes were molded to his binoculars, as they often were, and he was watching something across the yard.

"I'm sorry?" I called back.

"42," he repeated. "That's how many laps you've taken today."

"Were you counting?"

Without taking his eyes away from the scopes, he held one arm out. It was covered with tally marks checked in black permanent ink.

"That's weird, and I want to unsee that."

He shrugged.

"Why are we having this conversation?" I demanded.

"I just thought you should know they're looking for you."

A chilly breeze brushed my arms—but then again, that was the only kind of breeze they had around here. "They who?"

"I don't know, I can't read nametags from here. They're meeting with the big boss right now."

"How do you know they're looking for me?"

"Who else would they be looking for? You're the only criminal on this island worth the title."

"Thanks for the compliment, but this all sounds like a lot of conjecture. The United had me in prison for months on the mainland and barely talked to me. I don't think they're looking for me now."

He swiveled his binoculars to the other side of the yard. "All I'm saying is, you might want to lay low during dinner—and avoid government officials."

"I make a habit of it," I muttered, and resumed walking. "Stop me when I get to 50 laps."

Dinner was called before I completed my 46th lap. As I always did, I waited until almost everyone else had gone before joining the back of the line. My theory was that everyone would have already picked their seats by the time I got to the mess hall, and I could choose the most abandoned table.

Tonight, however, I was not so lucky. No sooner had I sat down than two old men got up from their table and came to join me.

I was appalled. Sure, there was no rule forbidding people from changing tables—I had just never seen anyone on this island exude that much effort.

"Hey Q! It's your buddy John!" the first one said.

"And Dowe!" the second echoed. "Remember us?"

I groaned. I *did* remember them, and that was the problem. This was the third time these fools had tried to introduce themselves to me, and the repetition was making it hard for me to block them from my memory.

It didn't help that their appearance was also very memorable, in a downright creepy way. John and Dowe were almost identical in height, hair, and weight, so much so that from across the yard you would swear they were twins. But when you got up close, you could spot just enough differences to know that they couldn't be related. Yet, they were joined at the hip and completed each other's sentences in a way that amplified their obnoxiousness.

"Much to my dismay," I returned. "But *you* seem to have forgotten that my name is not Q."

"Yeah, I'm not saying that," John retorted. "It takes too long."

"Sorry I'm such a test of patience."

"It's fine, he could use the practice." Dowe drained the last of his water and thumped his canteen on the table. "We've been looking for you, Q."

Tower's warning flashed through my mind. I eyed the curious pair, but I couldn't imagine them as government agents. Firstly, they were ancient. Secondly, they were dumb. Not in the inept, hive-mind way most United officials were—no, John and Dowe were *actually* stupid. I was sure some of it was an act, but the fact that they never broke character was disconcerting.

Best case scenario, they were harmless mental cases. Still, I would take any excuse to avoid them.

"I'm sorry, but my mom always told me never to talk to strangers."

"Don't worry, I left our big white van at home."

"Correction, you drove our big white van into the ocean six months ago."

"We can still get to it! It's stuck on a rock or something like ten yards out. I think we should turn it into a party space and rent it."

"What, so people can picnic on the roof?"

"Yeah!"

"I like the way you think."

"That's the entrepreneurial spirit," I inserted, hoping the interruption would derail the conversation permanently.

"We'll give you a cut if you advertise, Q."

"No thanks," I stood up and gathered my dishes, even though I hadn't had a chance to take a bite. "I've already got a job."

"So I heard."

I looked up sharply, but not quickly enough to see which one had spoken. "What did you hear?"

"Nothing definitive," Dowe answered. "But just in case, we wanted to cover our bases and make sure we got to you first."

Maybe Tower *was* talking about these two.

"I'm not interested," I snapped.

"Take it easy—we just wanted to give you this." Dowe pulled a crumpled piece of paper out of his pocket and tossed it at me.

I smoothed it out. It was a coupon for free pizza delivery. Expired, of course.

"Order whatever you want, on the house," John beamed.

"But it only works on the mainland," Dowe clarified. "Overseas shipping is too expensive."

"I'll save it for when I go on vacation." I crumpled it back up and dropped it on my tray.

"Hey, don't throw that away! It cost us an arm and a leg!"

"Yeah, Bob and Fred would be mortified."

"Dare I ask who Bob and Fred are?"

"When you see guys missing an arm and a leg, you'll know." Dowe held my gaze, dead-serious.

With the tips of my fingers, I gingerly picked up the coupon and stuffed it in the pocket of my jumpsuit, intending to throw it away or forget about it, whichever came first. "Well, thanks for the invigorating intellectual discussion, but I need to go…"

"Right, right. Hey, are you going to eat that?" Without waiting for an answer, John pulled my tray to himself and dug in.

"Nah, lost my appetite."

Neither of them appreciated the implications of that statement, so I left them to it and went to finish my laps.

"That's 50!" Tower called down to me. I saw him make another tally mark on his arm.

"Seriously, stop doing that."

"Who's the prisoner and who's the guard in this relationship?" He picked up his binoculars.

"Touché." I stopped beneath his tower. "By the way, you were right about them."

There was a pause. "Them?"

"John and Dowe," I clarified. "They found me. Again. I can't get rid of them."

He snorted. "I wasn't talking about them. They're friends."

"Well, that explains everything. So who *were* you talking about?"

He lowered his binoculars, revealing sunken raccoon eyes that were nearly hidden under a mess of unkept dark hair. "I was talking about Ambrose."

2

I immediately turned around and walked away.

"Where are you going?" Tower shouted after me.

"Following your advice—avoiding government officials."

Ambrose was a name I knew. I had seen it dozens of times in the form of a rubber stamp at the bottom of paperwork. Back when I had been the governor of a research base, Ambrose had been the supervisor of two scientists I wanted to recruit, which meant my transfer requests had to go through him. He had been a piece of red tape then—the all-powerful government figure whose hand I had to kiss if I wanted my paperwork approved.

We'd met in the flesh only once. He had been so gracious as to visit me in my first prison and lord his accomplishments over me. He claimed responsibility for putting me behind bars. I was quick to correct him and remind him that a Christian teenager—one of the many unassimilated, socially noncompliant reprobates his perfect government was supposed to be filtering out—was the one who turned me in. Ambrose just happened to be the recipient of her email and seized the profits. Credit where credit is due.

I could tell he wanted to kill me in exchange for my helpful fact-checking, but that would have required filing an incident report. I knew from experience how much paperwork that involved, and he decided I wasn't worth it.

I would have made the same choice, in his shoes.

I hadn't seen him since then. In fact, I hadn't seen much of anyone. Despite the fact that I'd been months away from staging a massive terrorist attack against the United, they hadn't been very interested in questioning me. You'd think they'd want to know how I'd almost managed to free *the entire planet of Mars* from United control, but apparently they didn't care, as long as I'd failed.

Which meant there was no good reason for him to track me all the way out here in the middle of the ocean.

I thought about giving him a chase—I could probably lose him in the unfinished factory for a few hours—but thought better of it. It was only a matter of time before they sent guards to haul me in, and if they discovered I wasn't in my cell after curfew, Ambrose would probably get to beat me free of charge.

I made it back to my cell just before the door automatically locked, signaling curfew. I turned out the light, slid the cover across the barred window of the door, and sat down at the desk to wait. I'm not sure why the cell had a desk—I hadn't seen a single book or piece of paper on the entire island—but sitting at the empty desk was slightly less dehumanizing than curling up on the weak cot that was too short for my lanky frame.

It wasn't ten minutes later that I heard heavy footsteps and winded breaths enter the corridor. He stopped outside my cell, blocking out the silver of light that crept in under the door.

"Let's talk," he said by way of introduction.

Let's not. I decided to ignore him, mostly just to see what he'd do.

"120518, I know you're in there."

What a Sherlock.

"Open the window."

Nah. I crossed my leg, leaned back in the chair, and waited.

He grunted and cussed. I heard keys rattle, then a swipe of a card in the door. It rejected him with a beep.

I couldn't resist a laugh into the darkness. They hadn't even given him access privileges.

He heard me and swore again. "Open up!"

"You want me to open the door from the inside? That's not how prisons work."

"Do it or I kill you."

"What kind of threat is that? You can't shoot me through the door, unless they gave you one of the good guns, but I don't think you have the clearance."

He mumbled into his communicator.

I lazily stood up and strolled to the door. "How pathetic. You have me in prison on the mainland for months—months!—and hardly say a word to me. Now you swim across the Atlantic to track me down, and you can't even get the door open."

I slid the cover back from the window, revealing an electric pistol aimed at the bars. I was right—it wouldn't have punctured the steel door. It was a child's weapon, really, perfectly suited to the childish man.

I put my hands up. "Please, go ahead. Shoot me. I've been waiting six months for one of you to have the courage."

He spat at me, but the spittle just landed on the handle of his own gun. He grimaced and wiped his hand on his pants.

"What do you want?" I asked. "It's past my bedtime."

He composed himself and put on a smile. "How are you liking Rott, 'Q'?" he slithered, lines clearly rehearsed.

"Don't even try. If you think I'm going to play that song and dance, you're wrong. Just tell me what you want so I can make a show of pondering your offer before slamming this shut in your face." I kept my hand on the window for emphasis.

"You're no fun. At least the Christians put on a good show."

"Then why don't you go back to supervising them, Ambrose? Go back to your cute little concentration camp with a cushy office and a dozen underlings to do your bidding. Go back to watching a bunch of spineless martyrs who don't have the gumption to scale a six-foot wall. Take the easy paycheck, you deserve it."

He was less bothered by that statement than I expected—probably because it was all true, and he didn't mind admitting it. "Maybe when I retire. Right now, though, I've received a better offer."

"Wonderful. I hope your promotion takes you far away from me."

"That is the only downside to this position—it dictates that you and I will be working very closely for the next few months."

"That tells me everything I need to know—I'm not interested, and goodbye."

I slid the window shut. He gave a startled noise I took some pleasure in.

"If you don't..." He swallowed the threat and reinstated his professionalism. "You haven't even heard the employee benefits yet."

"There's nothing you could offer me that would justify those working conditions."

He chuckled. "Really? There's nothing you want? Nothing at all that I could tempt you with? What *do* you want? Money? A state-of-the-art lab? Your own island?"

"I'd consider my own planet. If you offered me Mars, I'd probably play ball, but anything less than that—not interested."

"Your own planet, huh? I think that can be arranged."

"Oh really."

"Well, maybe not a whole planet but—"

"You're lying? How did I know."

"—I think we could spare a moon."

I walked back to the desk. He kept talking, his voice slightly muffled through the door. "We could set you up on a nice, deserted moon. Give you all the supplies you need to build your own self-sufficient base. Send a few scientists with you to keep you company. We couldn't give you interstellar travel, of course—you've proven you're not trustworthy with it—but we could abandon you to the stars to be the ruler of your own little kingdom."

I stopped, folded my arms, and waited for him to go away.

"That's what you want, isn't it? To be in control. To be free from government regulations and run your own life. To be alone."

I looked to the ceiling. "That last part is spot-on. Can I go to bed now?"

"I have the power. I know the people. I've been authorized to offer you whatever you want, if you'll just do one little project for me."

"And what project is that? What could I possibly offer you that would be worth such a price?"

He savored the moment a beat too long. "Red Rain," he cooed. "You could give us Red Rain, Dr. Nic."

3

My blood ran like fire and ice through my veins. I wasn't sure which reaction was more appropriate—abject horror, or unbridled rage. Mostly, I was annoyed that I hadn't seen it coming.

Of course the United wanted my beautiful weapon. Any overbearing government worth their salt would love to have it. It was genius—a compound of gases that, when combined with normal precipitation, condensed into an acid strong enough to melt metal. It was *the* perfect weapon.

Sadly, I had never been able to complete it; if I had, I wouldn't be in this mess. I would have beaten the United into submission, cut my base on Mars off from their control, and lived happily ever after. But the scientists who were supposed to be helping me design Red Rain got cold feet and turned it over to the government—or rather, their daughter did. She'd ratted me out to Ambrose, who'd been all too happy to alert the higher-ups and take the credit.

Now the United had all the research for my world-ending weapon—and probably all of my other inventions, too. I wondered what Philadelphia, with her self-righteous, cowardly morality, would think if she realized what she'd done when she involved Ambrose.

The emotions continued to vacillate in my mind, but I had no intention of wasting any of them on a subject as undeserving as Ambrose. "Well, that answers that question," I snapped, loud enough to be heard through the door. "No."

He struggled with a comeback for a minute. "You won't get a better offer."

"I also won't get a worse one."

"I can give you everything!" he screeched, stamping his foot like a toddler.

I stormed back to the door and scraped the window open. "Are you stupid? You can give me nothing."

He looked confused. "But the moon—"

"Do you know me so little? The moon means nothing to me if you have Red Rain. You can offer the whole galaxy and I still won't give you my weapon."

He was finally catching up. "Why do you care? We can't use it against you—not if you're on the moon."

I huffed. "I trust you about as far as I can throw you—but that's not what I'm worried about."

He guffawed. "So you're the altruistic one now, are you? Did prison give you a change of heart? Are you afraid some Christians are going to get hurt?"

"Don't bother me with morals. I just don't want you to have it."

"But why?" It was a genuine question. "Within a year you could be living on your own moon, completely free from our control. No rules. No red tape. No government looking over your shoulder or monitoring your phone calls. Why do you care what happens down here?"

He had a point—and to be fair, I didn't care. That had always been my plan: Cut myself off from Earth and leave the United to wallow in its tyranny until the heat death of the universe. I really didn't care what the United did to win its war; it would continue to commit atrocities with or without my weapon. But that didn't mean I was going to give it to them.

"Why, doctor?" Ambrose demanded. "Why won't you give me Red Rain?"

"Because I hate you," I said, and smiled.

He snarled. "Don't make me resort to threats."

"I think you're already past that stage—and threats of what? Will you finally kill me?"

"I'll put the paperwork in tonight."

"Great, I'll wait five years for it to be approved."

"Or I could just leave you here."

"You were going to do that anyway."

He grunted. I put my face to the bars, locking eyes with him to make sure I was understood. "You have nothing on me. If I refuse you, I go back to taking laps around the yard and pretend this conversation never happened."

He stepped back and eyed me over his nose—or he would have, had I not been a good five inches taller than him. "We'll see about that," he snapped, and turned to leave.

I waited until he had disappeared in the elevator before slamming the window shut in relief. I flopped back in the desk chair, exhausted. I had done more talking today than the last six months of my imprisonment combined, and not a single word had been intellectually stimulating.

I rolled Ambrose's threats around in my mind. If you weeded past the bravado, he had a point. He would be back, and he would bring the big guns. If the United was motivated enough to ship him across the ocean to find me, he wouldn't leave without a fight. He would try every trick in the book, and despite my nonchalance, I knew none of them would be pleasant.

Ambrose would do everything he could to make my life hell—and then, just maybe, he would be motivated to end it. And what if he didn't? What if I got my wish—to wander endlessly around this island until Tower tattooed his entire body with tally marks? Is that the best I could do?

I had no intention of giving the United Red Rain, and I was under no delusion that they'd give me the moon even if I did. But if I took their deal, they'd at least have to set me up in a lab somewhere. And maybe, just maybe, I could find a way to escape that didn't involve hitching a ride on a shark.

The longer I ran the numbers, the more I realized I didn't have anything to lose. If I failed, they would just kill me or send me back here, and I'd be no worse off than when I started. But at least, if I was on the mainland, I'd have a chance of getting the upper hand.

I liked those odds.

4

After breakfast, I started taking my laps like normal. I wanted to make Ambrose find me; I wasn't going to crawl to him sniveling.

It took him long enough. Lunch came and went, and I was a good twenty-five laps in for the day before he intercepted me.

"All right, Nic, let's talk. You want a planet? I've been authorized to consider it. You get us Red Rain, and we'll talk about Mars."

I was shocked. I had expected him to lead with threats, not more bribery. But I accepted it with a shrug. "Okay. Want to get coffee sometime?"

He jerked back. "What?"

"So we can talk details—it's too cold to be standing out here in this wind."

He wasn't there yet. "You… you want to talk?"

"Do I want to talk to you? No. Am I willing to? Yes."

He fumbled for a comeback and settled for honesty. "I'm… surprised, doctor."

"No one's more surprised than me. What can I say? Your speech yesterday—very convincing."

"You're kidding."

"About you being a convincing speaker? Of course I'm kidding. About being willing to negotiate? That's a genuine offer."

He squinted at me. "I don't trust you."

"Nor I you, but it seems we have found something in common—which, I hear, is the first step to friendship."

He bellowed a full-throated laugh. "That's rich."

"Like chocolate. Now. Shall we talk?"

He calmed himself. "I'm listening."

I had my list prepared. "I want a lab in North America, fully outfitted. I don't want to work with any Unionists, not even a secretary. I work my own way at my own pace—I don't want to hear anything about red tape or 'unapproved substances' or any of your other pomp and circumstance."

"Done," he said without batting an eyelash.

Those were the easy requests. "And I want my old assistant—Carnegie."

I didn't have to clarify who I meant. Ambrose's eyes flickered—he knew him. "I... I can't do that," he stuttered.

His nervousness was palpable, and that was deeply concerning. "Why not? He's a frail old man—he's no use to you."

Ambrose composed himself and plastered a cruel smile on his face. "Let's just say he's permanently unavailable."

I caught up. "Did you help him get there, or did he spare you the trouble?"

"It was a combined effort—made the paperwork much simpler."

"How considerate of him." I shook off the inconvenient emotion that threatened to invade my consciousness. "Fine. Then I'll work alone."

"As you wish."

"And one last thing."

He arched an eyebrow.

"I don't want to do any paperwork. Not a single report. I'll give you the work, but I'm not feeding your obsession with bureaucracy. I'll do the science, and I'll give you my progress updates verbally. If you make me do *any* kind of paperwork—and I mean any—the deal's off."

"You want me to put that in a contract?"

"Not if I have to sign it."

He grinned with the pent-up wickedness of a lifetime wasted on political ambition. "I'll see if I can pull some strings."

He started walking away. "Pack your bags, doctor. Our ship leaves in an hour."

I waited until he was out of sight before I resumed my walk. I had nothing to pack, and I was hoping that if I kept going in circles I could avoid John and Dowe. I was not interested in a goodbye.

There was one person I couldn't avoid, though, no matter where I went on the island. I kept my eyes straight ahead as I passed under Tower's post.

I heard his window open. "Hey, Q."

I reluctantly paused and looked up. Tower was staring into his binoculars, eyes elsewhere, but his voice floated down to me clearly. "A word of advice?"

"I collect them."

"If you reach a dead end—order pizza."

I remembered the expired coupon and came to the sad realization that Tower, John, and Dowe were just three peas in a pod. I continued walking. "I'll be sure to tell them who referred me."

*

It took more than an hour for our ship to leave—I'm sure something was wrong with the paperwork. Then came the idyllic two-day boat ride, during which Ambrose invested way too much energy in guarding me like he actually had to earn his paycheck. I'm sure he knew it was unnecessary; a pair of cuffs and a locked door would have done the job. Evidently he was trying to entertain himself, so I let him have it. He'd be out of my hair soon enough.

The boat ride was followed by a short trip up the East Coast in a helicopter. They blindfolded me when we neared the city so I wouldn't recognize it, not that it particularly mattered to me. I was herded into a van, which drove for another thirty minutes. Finally I was guided through a parking garage, up an elevator, and down a hall. There was a beep and a whoosh of a door being opened. Ambrose kicked me through, and then he finally removed the blindfold.

"Welcome home, doctor."

I glanced around the entryway, but there was nothing to see. "Save it for when you give me the moon."

He cackled. "I think you'll find the amenities sufficient. All of the research from your computers on Mars has been transferred to the databases. If you're missing anything essential, just put in a request through any computer terminal."

"What did I tell you about paperwork?"

He smiled. "I'll make sure to put your requests through on priority."

"Thank you for your attention to this matter."

He stepped out the door. "Get some rest. We'll touch base in the morning."

The door slid shut behind him, and I admired the control panel for it—it looked similar to the prototype door control system I had been testing on Mars. Of course, that system had its flaws—one of which ended up being my undoing.

I pushed the thought out of my mind and went to explore the amenities. It was nothing like my base on Mars, where I had unlimited space to build whatever facilities I needed, but it wasn't shabby. The United did have plenty of money, and apparently they were willing to throw some at this project.

The main lab was the first door down the hall to the left. It was well-stocked with the latest equipment, three computer stations, a gigantic digital whiteboard, and a sealed testing chamber.

A smaller, secondary lab was on the right, followed by the dorms. There were four small rooms attached to a combined bathroom/laundry room.

I opened the final door and found myself in a common room. It was connected to the main lab by a door, so you could easily walk back and forth from work to play. The room was cluttered with a recreational computer terminal, a couch, and a few tables and chairs. A small kitchenette was built into one wall, and the other was embedded with a vending machine. You could place an order for whatever you wanted, and it would be piped up from the cafeteria on another floor.

I patted my lean stomach, remembering the tar and plastic that had been considered "food" on Rott. Clearly, bargaining with Ambrose had its perks.

I walked over and tapped the screen, displaying a shockingly short menu of options. My disappointment fell as I tabbed through the dinner choices and realized I would not be dining on steak anytime soon.

No matter. I tabbed over to the drinks. As long as they had—

"Curse you, Ambrose." There was no coffee on the list.

I better get started on that escape plan right away.

5

I spent the first day looking through the data the United had stolen from me. It only took about ten minutes to determine that they'd copied my entire database; everything was exactly as I left it, except for a few paltry additions no doubt contributed by some inept United scientists.

Still, I wasted a whole day looking through it. The more time I could buy myself by pretending to be busy, the better.

The second day I wasted trying to hack onto another network. All the computers in the lab were connected to the same wifi. It could access the censored United internet, which was basically useless to me. United science was almost as bad as United politics, which meant, if I were going to do any real research, I needed to get onto some illegal sites.

More importantly, I was sure that the United was remotely monitoring everything that went on in the lab. It wasn't that hard for them; it was their wifi, and they had plenty of programs that did most of the work for them. If I had any hope of escaping, I needed to get onto another signal where I could speak a bit more freely.

Not that I had any idea who I would contact. Carnegie, my first choice, was dead. My other associates on Mars had likely fallen to similar fates, but even if they hadn't, none of them had the resources needed to truly help me. That left me with a few wealthy investors who might still owe me a favor for allowing them to conduct unsanctioned experiments on Mars. But wealth was a fickle thing, and now that I had none, they might not be so willing to honor their debts.

Although, at the rate I was going, it might not matter. Even though I found dozens of other wifi signals within range, I couldn't get onto any of them. I invested two whole days into the endeavor and had nothing to show for my efforts. Either the connections were very secure, or I was completely incompetent when it came to coding.

I knew the answer, not that I would have admitted it to anyone but myself. I'd almost blown my entire operation once by prematurely releasing a badly-coded computer virus. There had been two problems with that experiment. One, I didn't know enough about code to notice that the scientist behind it had intentionally written it wrong. And two, I'd been too dumb to realize that the network I was testing it on wasn't fully secure.

Thankfully, Carnegie had been around to help me clean up the mess. But that was a luxury I'd never have again.

I was moping over a boring dinner—pasta with plain tomato sauce (there wasn't an option to order cheese)—when the phone rang.

It wasn't a phone, per se—it was a communications program on the computer. A pop-up engulfed the screen, accompanied by a dorky ring that was probably a lame attempt at nostalgia.

I walked over to the terminal. I didn't recognize the number, and there was no profile picture—just an icon of the United's seal.

I rolled my eyes and accepted the call. "Good evening, Ambrose."

"Good guess, but this isn't Ambrose," a calm, calculated male voice answered.

"Well that just made my evening. To whom do I have the pleasure of speaking?"

"You can call me Thames, and trust me, there is absolutely no pleasure in our relationship."

"Suit yourself." I took another bite of pasta and spoke around it. "So how can I help you?"

"I'm a simple man—give me Red Rain, and I'll dance."

"Sounds great, but if you're expecting me to have it completed after only being here three days, then you need to learn a thing or two about science."

He snorted. "I know we can be demanding chaps up here in the office, but I'm not that stupid."

"Excellent. We'll get on fine, then—it's the stupid ones I can't stand."

"I'll do my best to meet your approval. In the meantime, give me your progress so far."

I chewed and swallowed another bite before answering. "I've started."

"That so? Because I haven't seen a single change to the database, and I don't believe you've been granted paper privileges."

The pasta landed like a lump of coal in the pit of my stomach. "There's a whiteboard..."

He sighed. "Doctor, I don't enjoy these conversations any more than you do, so I'm going to make it easy on both of us and keep it simple. Either you start working, and you work hard, or I'll kill you."

"I think I liked Ambrose better—at least he had the decency to banter a bit before he issued the death threats."

"Perhaps that's why Ambrose is still working for me, instead of the other way around. In any case, I'll check on you tomorrow evening. I hope you have a better story for me then."

He hung up without ceremony. I aggressively stirred my pasta around my plate. "Oh don't you worry, I will," I mumbled to the empty room.

The next day, I did my best to work without working. I modified databases, fiddled with equations, and ran simulations—all of which I'd run before on Mars. The results were all the same, but at least it generated a fresh wave of data to satisfy Thames.

When he called that evening, I did my best to sell the work I had done. This was a skill I was actually quite good at. When you're soliciting investors for a project that is entirely theoretical, you have to be able to sell a concept rather than a product. Each test and simulation can represent a golden breakthrough if you stage it right.

Thames seemed to buy my advertising. He left me with another threat to get me through the day, then hung up. I spent the next day fudging, and we repeated this song and dance for two weeks.

While my pointless tests were running, I continued to scour the internet, looking for any lifeline. I looked up my old investors; unsurprisingly, all of them had changed their contact information after the government busted my base. I looked for information on my sister Cea but found nothing current. I tried looking up Thames and discovered he was fairly high up the political food chain—which meant literally every scrap of information on him was classified.

I knew they could see all of my internet activity, but at this point, I wasn't sure it mattered. I was getting nowhere.

It was also becoming increasingly harder to fake work. I had already put nearly a decade of my life into this project, and that was coming back to bite me. I had been working for years to come up with the formula for Red Rain, which meant there was literally nothing I had not tried. I had run every test and every simulation and used every program known to mankind. I had hundreds, if not thousands, of failed chemical sequences. And, unfortunately, being in prison hadn't made me any smarter—all the problems that had stumped me before continued to perplex me. I was no closer to completing my weapon than I ever was.

All this meant that there was only so much work I could fake, so many tests I could repeat, before it became obvious even to a non-scientist that I was copying and pasting.

I could tell by the way my conversations with Thames were getting shorter and shorter and his voice was getting colder and colder that I was reaching the end of the line with him. But I knew I was done for when he called twice in one day.

"Back so soon? You must really love me." I was attempting attitude, but the words came out limp.

"Don't worry, I won't keep you. I don't want to take up your evening."

"How considerate. I was just about to watch one of your inane censored TV shows. I really love the part where everyone's stupid."

"Same. Anyway, I just called to tell you—we have your sister in a concentration camp."

He said it like a threat, but I didn't take it as one. "Which is where she should be, according to your hierarchy. She is too religious for your tastes—and mine, most of the time."

"She doesn't have to stay there."

"You could send her to Rott—tell her I'll meet up with her when you get tired of dealing with me."

"I mean I could kill her, Nic."

"I knew what you meant," I muttered, but my boisterous sarcasm died halfway through the sentence. It was a cheap shot on Thames's part, but well-aimed. I had never been under any delusions that Cea was safe with the United, but I had never intended to use her as my scapegoat.

Thames was content to let me ponder that threat in silence for a moment. I weighed the odds. It had only been two weeks, and Thames was already resorting to his trump card. That meant I didn't have a lot of time before he put me—and Cea, apparently—on the chopping block. In the meantime, I was no closer to figuring a way out of here.

If I was going to get out of this alive, I needed to buy myself more time. That meant Thames had to see real progress, which was something I couldn't give him.

But I knew someone who could.

It was time to pull out *my* trump card: Blame somebody else.

But for that to work, I knew I had to sell it. You can't just cast blame around like confetti; if you wanted it to stick, you had to prime the wall.

"Listen, Thames. I'm going to tell you something that will blow your mind."

"Please don't."

"The truth."

The line went silent. I modulated my voice to make it sound like I'd had a change of heart. "I can't complete Red Rain."

"Really? What finally gave it away? The two weeks of crushing failure?"

I laughed. "I knew before I even set foot in this lab."

He didn't respond.

"Don't you get it?" I jeered. "I knew I couldn't complete the formula. I've known that for years. I just wanted to get off that putrid island. I figured I could string you along for a while until I figured out a way to escape... but I see you don't have that kind of patience."

"You expect me to believe that?" he spat in a way that suggested he might.

"No." I let the silence bake for a beat. "But you might, if I gave you the man who *could* complete the formula."

"If you were lonely and wanted a roommate, you could have just said something. Who is it?"

With a smile he sadly couldn't see, I whispered, "Smyrna."

"The girl?" he sputtered.

The girl? You mean Philadelphia? It was so absurd that I cackled. Since when had that obnoxious brat become the most famous member of her family?

Although, when I considered it, it made some sense. After all, she was the one who had cozied up to the government and dropped the hint about my project. She had probably become a household name around the office.

The memory of her stupid doe-eyes caused my fists to tighten, but I kept the bitterness out of my voice as I continued to lead Thames along. "Yes, of course I mean Phil—she's a chemical genius, didn't you know? No, you moron, I mean the old man. Dr. Thomas Smyrna. If you want this project complete, he's the one you want."

"Prove it."

That was easy. "Why do you think I summoned him to Mars? Do you know how much that cost? How much red tape I had to hurdle? You politicians do not make it easy to reassign unassimilated. You think I would go through all that trouble if I didn't think he could do it?"

"You said the same thing about Ephesus once."

"Ephesus and I had a labor dispute. He probably could have done it, but he didn't like my benefits package." With a dry chuckle, I realized how true that was. I cleared my throat. "However, I don't think you'll have that problem."

"Fine," he said after a pause. "I'll bring him in. But you're not going anywhere until I have a complete formula. I don't care who does the work—just make it happen, or I'll kill all of you."

"I'd expect nothing less," I said, and hung up.

6

I tried to tidy up the place—and myself—before going to bed. I knew I was essentially a caged lab rat, but at least I didn't have to look like one. As far as the old man was concerned, I ran this lab, and I was very comfortable doing it.

Thames, for all his flaws, wasn't a procrastinator, and my victim was delivered early the next morning. I heard the commotion coming down the hall and staged myself right inside the door. My lab coat was freshly bleached, and I had my mug posed in my hand. The effect would have been better had there been something other than water in the cup, but the old man would probably be too flabbergasted to notice anyway.

I put on my most commanding smile as the door slid open. "Welcome to the... what are *you* doing here?"

Ephesus stood in the hall. He had apparently not come willingly; two burly guards were at his elbow. He threw both of them off to lunge at me.

There was nowhere to run in the narrow entryway, so he succeeded in slamming me against the wall. I dropped my cup, spilling the contents all over my coat. "Good thing that wasn't coffee," I hissed at him.

In typical Smyrna fashion, he wasn't listening. His hands were cuffed, but that didn't stop him from putting them around my throat.

"What are you doing here? Answer me!" he screeched as he attempted to throttle me.

I drew my knee back and kicked him where it hurt. He stumbled backward into the guards, who were kind enough to restrain him.

"This is my lab," I huffed. "And I asked you first."

His face twisted, like he couldn't decide whether being confused or angry was more important. "What do you mean? You called me here!"

"I did no such thing! I haven't needed you in two years, and you know it."

He did know it, which shut him up, at least for the moment.

"It's your father I want."

"I'm here." He emerged from the hall. He wasn't cuffed, which said volumes about the situation. "Care to explain what's going on?"

"You and I are here to work. Him?" I jabbed a finger at his son. "I have no idea." I gestured at the guards. "Take him back. He'll only get in the way."

They shrugged. "Thames's orders."

I groaned. "Of course they are."

The guards released Ephesus's cuffs and unceremoniously dropped him on the floor, then promptly left, locking the door behind them. Ephesus took a moment to orient himself before springing back into action.

"All right, you, let's finish this."

I cast a bored look at Smyrna. "Control your son. What a disgrace."

"Enough, both of you," he said in a voice that indicated he hadn't slept all night. He certainly looked like he hadn't slept in a week, or maybe a year. "Before anybody throws any punches, I think we need to hear the full story. What's going on? Why are you here?"

"Yeah, how are you still alive?" Ephesus brushed himself off. "I figured they would have executed you."

"Ephesus," Smyrna scolded.

I laughed. "Too much paperwork. Prison is a much easier legal process. And I was rather enjoying the reprieve—until they realized they couldn't survive without my genius."

"Spare me."

"What can I say? They saw how brilliant Red Rain was and demanded to have it for themselves."

They responded with stunned silence, and I realized that may not have been the best way to introduce the project.

"You've got to be kidding me," Ephesus exclaimed, and the look in his eyes said that he hoped it really was a joke.

Smyrna muttered something that was a cross between an oath and a prayer.

"I wish I was, young man, but I'm afraid the terms are very simple: Either we collectively put our genius together and give them the completed formula for Red Rain, or we die." I shrugged.

Ephesus balled his fists, but Smyrna put his hand up. His eyes locked with mine. "Show me."

I led them to the main lab. Smyrna sat down in front of a computer terminal and started riffling through the databases. His son read over his shoulder.

"It's all here," Ephesus breathed after a minute. "Every bomb and gun I ever created for you—it's all here. And you gave it all to *them*!"

"I didn't 'give' them anything. They stole it."

He wasn't interested in the semantics. He screamed, a primal yell of pure rage. He drew his arm back, but for once, his fist wasn't aimed at me. He turned to the nearest wall and slammed his entire body weight into the plaster—one, two, three times.

"Ephesus," the old man tried.

Ephesus gave another punch, weakly this time, then leaned his head against the wall. "This is all my fault."

"That's a bit of a stretch," I said.

He traced his finger around the hole he'd created in the drywall. "I never should have bargained with you. I never should have made *anything* for you. I should have made you kill me."

I shrugged. "Probably."

Smyrna frowned at me. "What did they tell you? What do they want?"

"Red Rain, obviously." I took the other desk chair. "Apparently when they raided my base, they decided to keep my work for themselves. Philadelphia did them a favor, really."

Ephesus turned. "Leave my sister out of this!"

"She's already involved," Smyrna said, so quietly I was lucky to hear him. He shared a heavy-handed look with Ephesus.

The kid washed white.

"What?" I said, suddenly very concerned that there was something I should know. I hated that feeling.

"Conveniently, Phil was taken into 'special custody' last night," Ephesus snapped. "Now I know why." The anger returned to his eyes, but they burned a different shade of black now.

"I don't know anything about that," I scoffed, even though I definitely did. As I suspected, Thames *did* know how to assemble a good "employee benefits" package.

Smyrna turned back to me. "What other demands did they give you? Any deadlines?"

"You know how they are—it's all blood and death and totalitarianism. They haven't set a deadline, but Thames's patience only lasted about two weeks with me, so I'd personally recommend 'sooner' rather than 'later.'"

"This 'Thames' character—he's in charge?" Ephesus asked.

I turned the chair to face him. "His one claim to fame."

"Let me guess." Ephesus crossed his arms. "He called your bluff—you don't know how to complete Red Rain—so you threw us under the bus to buy yourself some time."

I grinned. "That's why I always liked you, Ephesus—you're smart. You know, in another lifetime, we could have been great friends."

"Thanks, but I don't plan on seeing you in the next lifetime."

Smyrna looked appalled. I thought it was hilarious. Where had this Ephesus been all my life? "Guess we'll have to get all our male bonding done in this lifetime, then."

He rolled his eyes. "I really hate you."

"Tell me something I don't know."

"I'm not working on Red Rain."

"Again, I'm waiting…"

He ignored me. He strode over to his father and leaned on the desk. "Dad, you stall them. Fiddle with the formula and make it look like you're making progress—buy me a few days. I'll hack around in the computer and see what I can find out. We need to get out of here before this Thames guy gets bored."

"I like this plan," I said, not that they'd asked.

Smyrna tentatively laid his hands on the keyboard. "But what about Philadelphia? If Thames thinks we're planning something, she'll take the fall."

Ephesus searched his father's face. "I'll see if I can figure out where they're keeping her," he said, which didn't answer the question.

"You," he straightened and turned to face me, "are going to help me hack out of here."

"I thought you'd never ask. I know just the place to start." I stood up and gestured with my arm, and he followed me to the common room.

"The vending machine? Are you serious?" he muttered when I gestured to the cursed object.

I tapped the screen. "It's locked to a limited—and entirely tasteless—menu. I want you to hack it so we can order whatever we want."

Ephesus sighed, but the sound was more tired than angry. For a flicker of a moment, he looked uncannily like his father.

"Can't you take anything seriously? Is that a function your brain possesses?"

"You can't order coffee."

He blinked. "I'll get right on it."

7

Smyrna also got "right on it." Out of sheer boredom, I went to check on him a few hours later and found that he had completely reorganized and recategorized the entire Red Rain database. All of the backups the inept government officials had carelessly copied were now properly synced and labeled. When I approached, he was converting some of my redundant lab test results into a usable report.

"Slow up, old man," I said with as much genuine appreciation as I dared give him, "or they'll expect this kind of pace all the time."

"How *do* you work like this?" He gestured at the computer.

"That's just it—I wasn't working."

He arched one eyebrow and resumed typing.

"But... my real databases are almost as bad. That's why I needed Carnegie."

"No wonder you never finished the project," he muttered.

"Hey, I don't need that level of violence from you, old timer." I leaned against the desk and watched him work for a minute. "So, what do you think?"

"About what?" he said without looking up.

"The data. My idea." I jabbed my finger at the diagnostics he had pulled up. "Red Rain. Can it be done?"

"You asked me that once before."

"And you never gave me a straight answer—your daughter quite rudely interrupted us with her theatrics."

He almost smiled.

"So? What do you think?"

He paused mid-keystroke and stared at the screen. I could tell by the way his eyes were flickering back and forth that he was reading, processing.

I leaned over and tapped the monitor, navigating to a new folder. I pulled up a different report and enlarged it, then sat back and waited.

I had been through this process dozens of times. Each time I invited a new scientist to join the project, I showed them the data and asked for their verdict. Their answer determined whether or not they would be allowed access. As they studied the data, I watched their faces, searching not only for intelligence but also for faith.

Ah, faith—such a double-edged sword. Faith in religion was a stumbling block. Faith in the government was a death sentence. But faith in science—it was essential. I needed them to believe in the project. I needed them to believe it could be done. If I saw doubt and rejection in a scientist's eyes, I disqualified them from the project, no matter how brilliant their test scores.

That was why I had liked Ephesus, at first—he believed everything could be done until proven otherwise. To his credit, I don't think he ever stopped believing in Red Rain. In fact, it was his faith in the project that was his undoing—he *did* believe it could be done, and that scared him.

I expected the father to be much the same way. Still, I was more than a little gratified when I saw that telltale flicker of curiosity burn in his eyes.

It extinguished when he leaned back and sighed. "In theory, I suppose," he said after he took a painfully long moment to filter his thoughts. He glanced at me. "But I won't do it for you."

I stood up. "I wasn't asking."

I returned to the common area to find Ephesus rebooting the vending machine. He glanced over his shoulder and beckoned to me. "Here, try it now."

I grabbed an abandoned mug from the table and set it on the dispenser. I tapped the screen and was delighted when a whole menu of options popped up. I found coffee, selected the blackest setting, and hit dispense.

Both Ephesus and I held our breaths. After a minute of contemplation, the machine gurgled, and a stream of freshly brewed coffee sizzled into the cup.

Ephesus muttered congratulations to himself. I waited until the mug filled, then took a swig, welcoming the burn on my tongue. As the life-giving fluid rushed through my veins, I contemplated nirvana and wondered if this was what it felt like to be a normal, balanced human.

"You know what your problem is, Ephesus?"

He spared me a sideways glance as he screwed the access panel back on.

"You never should have gone into engineering. Hacking is clearly your true calling."

He acknowledged the truth of that with a half-smile. "Well, hopefully I'm good enough to hack our way out of here." He fetched a clean mug and made a cup of coffee for himself, although his had more cream and sugar than I thought healthy.

I sat down at the table and waited for him to join me. He took a swig and then leveled his gaze on me. "So what really happened? Have you been in prison this whole time?"

"No, I've actually been on vacation in the Bahamas."

"You should have worked on your tan—you look paler than usual."

"First of all, I don't tan, I burn. Second of all, of course I've been in prison. What else were they going to do with me?"

He shrugged. "Which prison?"

"What's it to you?"

He spread his hands. "I'm just trying to figure out what's going on. And I'm morbidly curious."

"Well, I wish I could give you all the gory details of their torture routine, but in reality, it was quite dull. It's an island, and absolutely no one of import was imprisoned there."

"Such humility."

"You know, I think I liked you better when you were too scared to talk back to me."

"The good old days. But how did you get here?"

"Ambrose found me," I said with no ceremony at all, and waited for his reaction.

His eyes flared. "Ambrose! So he guards a prison island now?"

"No, apparently he's a big shot under Thames." I sipped my coffee. "My guess? He got a promotion because he tipped them off about Red Rain after your sister alerted him."

Mentioning Philadelphia was unnecessary—I just added it to annoy him, which it did. However, he didn't argue. "So what do you know about Thames?"

"Absolutely nothing. I haven't even met him. We've only spoken on the phone."

"Mysterious," Ephesus muttered, which it kind of was.

"He's got money and influence, so I'm guessing he's either a politician or has bought a few off, and I suppose that's really all we need to know about him."

Ephesus nodded and swirled his coffee around in his cup. "And what about this lab? What do you know about the building? Do other people work here? How busy is it?"

"Again, absolutely nothing," I admitted. "They blindfolded me on the way in—something about a grand reveal."

"I hope someone brought confetti." He leaned back in his chair. "They brought us in the back of a van. This place isn't very far from camp—we were only driving for maybe 20-30 minutes."

That was important information; the proximity to the camp probably meant Ambrose and Thames had a preexisting professional relationship. However, I wasn't sure this revelation helped us at all.

Although, if we were close to the concentration camps, that meant we were also close to Cea—a prospect I hadn't considered before.

"They brought us through a parking garage and then up an elevator—so we're up at least a couple stories," Ephesus continued. "What we need to find out is how many other people work in this building, and what the security's like. That's how we'll know the best way to break out of here."

"Your best bet is to try and hack onto another wifi connection. There are several nearby."

"Have you been able to get onto any of them?"

It was asked without malice, but I ignored the question. "If you can see what kind of activity there is on the other networks, that should tell you how busy the building is."

He searched me for a moment, then decided it wasn't worth the effort. "I'll see what I can do. Meanwhile, I need you to try and build a bomb."

A comeback leapt to my tongue immediately, but it took me several beats to comprehend what he was implying. "Why would I need to build a bomb? You've already designed dozens."

"I'm well aware—I need you to construct a prototype of one. I'm sure you can scrouge up enough material in this lab to string something together."

"I'm sure," I returned, "but why?"

"First, it'll buy us some time if it looks like you're doing actual work. Maybe if they see you doing something constructive, they'll assume we've 'seen the light' and are being compliant. Second..." He let out a courage-rallying breath. "I'm sure we're going to need it."

"I'm sure we will."

I drained the last of my coffee contemplatively. When I lowered my cup, I found him gawking at me. "What? Is my mustache not even?"

"I mean, kinda," he said, "but I was expecting you to argue."

"It is?" I reached up and felt it with both hands. "Cheap razor…"

"Nic."

I met his gaze. "It's not rocket science. I don't want to die. And if busting out with you is my best chance at life—and, to my dismay, I think it's my only chance, based on all the available data—then, well: Whatever you say, captain."

He hummed contemplatively and stood up. "I can accept that."

"I strongly recommend that you do—because it's also *your* only chance of getting out of here alive."

He left me with a cold-hearted glare as he walked out of the room.

8

For the next two days, our strange little threesome hummed with harmony. I stayed out of everyone's way and made a bomb—two of them in fact. The first one was a dud (thankfully I didn't set off the smoke alarms), but the second would suffice.

It was harder than I would have expected. Despite being in a lab full of chemicals, I had to jerry-rig some obscure ingredients—several of which I got off the vending machine—to make anything even remotely explosive. It was almost like Thames had planned it that way, but I wasn't sure he deserved that much credit.

Ephesus, meanwhile, hacked onto several of the other wifi networks. It took him the rest of the day to do it, which made me feel slightly less incompetent—but only slightly.

He quickly determined that the building we were in was very busy, nearly around the clock, but not with other lab work. Most of the activity seemed to be mundane office traffic—computers, cellphones, and even a live printer that used real paper.

What was strange was how highly secured everything was. Ephesus claimed he was having trouble hacking into any of the devices or shared databases on the networks. He spent the whole second day trying and failing. And since he had no trouble admitting defeat—unlike myself—I knew he was being completely honest.

It wasn't difficult to connect the dots. Clearly we were in a government building of some kind. For a government that demanded uninhibited access to all its citizens' information, they sure did know how to keep their own stuff secure.

Ephesus also failed to find out any information about Philadelphia. I personally wasn't worried. I knew how the United operated; as long as Smyrna continued to make progress, they would gladly sit on their hands and wait. Phil was probably languishing in a cell somewhere, bored out of her mind but completely unharmed.

Out of curiosity, I had Ephesus run a search on Cea. Her record claimed she was still at the containment camp—but then again, so did Phil's.

Smyrna, for his part, was putting on a great show for anyone who might be watching the computer log. In two days he did an astounding amount of work without actually accomplishing anything. Every byte of data on Red Rain was converted and reformatted and converted again. He created tables, repositories, and even a pie chart. Currently he was working on putting together a formal scientific paper about the project. Anyone who wasn't a scientist would easily believe that great progress was being made.

The phone was pleasantly silent; it wasn't until after lunch on the third day that Thames decided to check in.

I was close to a terminal, having dropped into the lab to keep Smyrna company, so I answered. "I thought you'd forgotten about me, Thames."

"Put Smyrna on the line," he demanded without any kind of greeting.

At the mention of his name, Smyrna looked up from the monitor.

I took a chug from my third cup of coffee for the day. "Wow, so I'm not the favorite child anymore. I see how it is."

"Put Smyrna on the line," he repeated, "or I'll send a technician up there to 'fix' the vending machine."

I swallowed my mouthful very slowly.

Smyrna rolled his desk chair over to the terminal. "I'm here."

"Let me know when Nic has left the room."

Smyrna looked up at me. I raised my hands in surrender. "Fine, I'll text you later."

I walked out into the hall, shut the door behind me, and stubbornly leaned against the wall to wait.

Ephesus found me a few minutes later and questioned me with a raised eyebrow.

I jabbed my finger at the lab. "Thames wanted to have a one-on-one with your father."

All of his features darkened. He strode up to the door and tried it, only to find it locked.

We waited there together, Ephesus tensed like a tiger ready to strike, for another five minutes. Finally, the doors parted, revealing the old man leaning on the frame. He looked winded, like the conversation had taken everything out of him.

"Dad!" Ephesus was in his face. "What happened? Are you all right?"

"Thames just wanted an update," he replied, ignoring the latter question.

"And?" I prompted.

His eyes met mine, but his expression was uncategorizable.

"Dad, what did he tell you?"

"I'm supposed to tell you—" his gaze shifted to Ephesus and back again, "—both of you that he has Cea in solitary."

I wasn't sure which was more disturbing—this revelation, or the fact that Ephesus was exponentially more distraught about it than I was. "Cea! She was the other arrest. Oh no..."

"It's his funeral," I huffed. "Cea has probably made him regret that choice several times already."

Neither seemed consoled by this nugget of humor.

Ephesus kicked his feelings aside and turned his attention back to his father. "What else did he say?"

Smyrna shook his head.

"Dad."

"He asked about progress—"

"Dad," Ephesus grunted, "there's no way he called just to tell you about Cea."

"Agreed," I said, laying on the pressure. "And, to my chagrin, I must remind you that whatever he told you affects all of us."

Smyrna's eyes snapped to mine again. This time, his expression was clearly one of anger and hate.

"Dad," Ephesus tried one more time, "what is it?"

"Well, we already knew he had Philli," he snapped, the bitterness in his voice still matching the expression on his face. He turned to his son, then immediately looked down and away, as if regretting that decision.

"We should get back to work," he mumbled. "And watch what you say—if Thames knows about the vending machine, he probably knows about other things."

He stood back and shut the door to the lab before either of us could ask any more clarifying questions.

Ephesus turned to me with a raised eyebrow. I decided to answer the easy question first. "He threatened to take away my coffee." I contemplated the bottom of my empty cup. "And, I'm no psychologist, but based purely on your father's uncharacteristic display of emotion, I suspect he threatened to take away some other things, too."

"I'll talk to him later," Ephesus said, and I wondered if he actually would. "In the meantime, we'd better iron out the kinks in our escape plan."

I followed him to the common area. He turned on the cafeteria computer and pulled up a blueprint.

"I found this schematic of the building. It's back from when the construction project was originally approved, so it's probably not completely current, but close enough."

I glanced at it; it was a typical office layout, with an elevator on either side of the building and stairwells on the opposite ends.

"Unfortunately, according to these plans, the only floors that could accommodate a lab this size are fifth and ninth—which means blowing a hole in the wall and jumping for it is not an ideal option."

"Good, because I don't like that plan anyway. Any other ideas?"

"Well, the good news is I think I found a way to unlock all the doors at once."

I blinked. "Run that by me again."

"It's not as miraculous as you think. Because this building isn't normally used as a prison, it has the typical safety features of a public building—namely, if the fire alarm goes off, all doors immediately unlock so that everyone can have free access to the emergency exits."

"So what's the problem? Anyone can set off a smoke alarm."

"Yes, but there's a delay. The smoke alarm will run for a few minutes—then, if no one yells 'I'm just cooking!' it will assume there's a fire and enact the emergency protocols throughout the building."

"Okay," I said, chagrined that I was clearly missing the obvious flaw.

"I guarantee you, if we set off the smoke alarm on this floor, all the guards will come running."

"As they should," I admitted. I thought for a minute. "So let's blow them up with one of my bombs."

Ephesus cracked a smile. "Precisely. I think we should lure them into this room and plant a bomb on that wall." He turned and pointed to the far corner. "An explosion should create more than enough cover for us to slip out one of these doors."

He was right—the common room had two entrances, one to the lab and one to the hall. No matter which door the guards came in, we wouldn't be cornered.

"I'm sold. When do we leave? I'm free next Tuesday."

"I think we should do it after-hours—the fewer people that can respond, the better. But *when* is not really the issue."

I lifted an eyebrow and waited.

"The issue is where do we go after we get out."

"I recommend far away from here."

"Agreed, but as soon as we break out, we'll be wanted criminals. We're not going to be able to show our faces anywhere within a 30-mile radius, and if they flag our prints, we won't be able to use computers at all. We need a place we can go, preferably off the grid, while we try to find our sisters."

He had a point—and I was fresh out of off-the-grid sanctuaries at the moment. "Too bad we don't have access to a remote scientific base on a distant planet."

He glared at me but continued. "I have some ideas, but I need more time. Trouble is I can't just 'make a call' from any of these computers—I'm sure they can track all the internet usage in this building, even on the other networks. I have to find another way to contact my friends."

"But you do have friends," I clarified.

He let out his breath. "I hope so."

"Must be nice."

"You should try it sometime."

"Maybe when I have more free time." I got up to refill my coffee. "So what do we do?"

"I think we have a few days. They just threatened us—they'll give us some time to comply before they up the ante. As long as Dad continues to fake progress, I don't think they'll pull the trigger." He paused. "But in the meantime, another bomb wouldn't hurt."

I took a slow drag of coffee. "They never do."

9

Ephesus locked himself in the secondary lab and emerged only for dinner. I took over the common room and started building another bomb on the kitchen counter.

It proved much harder than the first two, primarily because several of the ingredients I needed were no longer available on the vending machine. Was the kitchen merely out of stock, or had the ingredients been intentionally removed? If Thames knew what I was doing, you think he would have sent someone to dispose of the bomb I already made.

I tried not to think too much of it and instead put my PhD in chemical engineering to the test as I tried to concoct another explosive equation. It was past midnight when I finally felt ready to make a prototype.

I opened the door to the adjoining lab and walked in. I started rooting through the scientific paraphernalia on the table, tossing what I didn't need on the floor.

"What do you need?"

I'm not pleased to report that the sudden declaration made me jump. I hadn't realized Smyrna was still in the lab. He was standing in front of the digital whiteboard, a red marker in his hand. He turned his head only slightly to acknowledge me.

"I could ask you the same question. Have you left this lab at all today? Do you need water? Food? A potty break?"

He looked like he needed all three—plus a shower and a week of sleep. The dark circles turned his face into a raccoon's, and his eyes looked like they had been murdered. They were bloodshot beyond recognition and swam with either fatigue or tears—maybe both.

"Seriously, old man, you need a break."

"I'm fine," he snapped. "I need to finish this."

"What's the rush? The United doesn't expect you to work 24/7. There's always tomorrow."

"Not always. Are you done?" His eyes shifted to my armload of gadgetry.

I passive-aggressively grabbed three more things—even though I didn't need them—and retreated back to the common room.

My bomb was a flop. Thankfully it didn't misfire; it failed to ignite at all, and the only explosion was the eruption of curses I let out. By then, it was almost 2 AM, so I gave up and went to bed.

Ephesus had long since been asleep. If Smyrna ever came to bed, I didn't hear him, and his dorm was empty when I got up.

Ephesus made a brief appearance to get breakfast before returning to his work. I reworked my chemical equation, and by mid-afternoon I was ready to make another prototype.

This one also failed to ignite, but the problem was one I thought I could solve. I needed another tool from the lab.

This time, I opened the door and looked in before entering. Somewhat to my surprise, Smyrna wasn't around. There was an abandoned plate and cup on the desk, so he had at least stopped to eat at some point. Maybe he had finally given up and gone to the bedroom to pass out.

It wasn't hard to tell where he had left off: The whiteboard, which was nearly ten feet long, was completely covered in scribbles. Several markers lay uncapped on the tray.

I walked over to it. What could he have been working on that was so urgent? He was only supposed to be faking work, and the whole idea of fake work was that there wasn't a deadline.

I scanned the board, and at first, I had no idea what I was looking at. It was a chemical equation, but his work was a mess of notes and half-finished sequences and revisions on the above— some numbers crudely hashed out and rewritten two or three times.

What was this for? Had he simply barfed random engineering nonsense onto the board to make it look like he was busy? There's no way that would have kept him up all night.

I took a step back so I could see the whole picture. I started in the corner of the board and read the entire sequence, then read it again, and again. Bits and pieces started to look familiar. I recognized the components and strung the chain reaction together in my mind. I combined the molecules and visualized the compound forming—and suddenly, I knew what I was looking at.

This was the formula for Red Rain.

The *real* formula. Not a dummy equation strung together to put on a façade of progress—this was functional science. Smyrna had done it. He had finished Red Rain.

Well, almost finished. The formula needed some polishing; the equations needed to be condensed and simplified, and the sequence wasn't quite complete. But this was further than I'd ever gotten, and I was confident that, given enough time, Smyrna could complete the project.

A decade of aspirations culminated in one wild, drunken burst of elation. My project was a success. Every hope I'd left to die on the sand at Rott came rushing back—cutting myself off from the United, defending my own planet, kicking the government where it hurt. I could do it. I could still win.

Except for one problem: This was a government lab, which meant the United now had Red Rain, too.

I cussed and examined the whiteboard. A quick browse of the settings menu showed that it wasn't wifi-enabled; it was, essentially, a big piece of scrap paper.

I let out my breath in relief. That meant Smyrna's scribbles weren't synced to any databases. I needed to download the screen capture to something portable, then erase the board before anyone else got ahold of it.

I ran to the desk and started rifling through the computer paraphernalia. There had to be some device I could use. Maybe Ephesus could hack one of the tablets and take it off the wifi so it couldn't be monitored.

Just then, the phone rang.

It took three rings for me to compose myself. I hastily answered and hoped my voice sounded as disinterested as usual. "The renowned Dr. Nic speaking."

"Where's Smyrna?"

I hesitated, then realized the truth was the safest answer. "I actually have no idea. I think he finally took a much-needed siesta. He was up *all* night working for you. You'd be so proud." I laid that last part on thick, hoping the implication of progress would satisfy him.

"Oh I know," he replied. "He told me."

My blood ran cold.

Thames didn't wait for a reaction. "Tell him my representative will be there at five to review the report."

There was a beat, but Thames kept talking before I could fully appreciate how my world had just ended. "By the way," he added, "I owe you an apology, doctor. You were telling the truth about the old man."

He hung up before I could thank him for his humility.

I stumbled back from the monitor. I dug my hands in my hair, taking a few strands out by the roots, and swore over and over and over into the empty room. It did nothing to relieve the tension.

Thames knew about Red Rain. Smyrna must have called him late last night. And how he was sending someone to retrieve the data.

It wasn't supposed to be this way. Smyrna was supposed to take the fall for my failure—receive the brunt of Thames's anger, die if he had to. He wasn't supposed to *give* them my weapon.

I'd rather die than let the United have Red Rain. Which meant we had to move, and now.

I wiped my palms on my coat. Returning to the desk, I started hurling devices on the floor until I found one I could use: An orange flash drive. Ephesus's initials were written on the scuffed surface. It was old, which meant it was unlocked—just what I needed.

I jammed it in the computer and copied over anything I thought I might need. Then I took it to the whiteboard, plugged it in, and saved the contents of the screen to the drive. After double- and triple-checking to make sure it had copied, I used my hand to hastily wipe the board clean.

Putting the drive in my pocket, I opened the door to the common area and looked in. Neither Ephesus nor the old man was there.

I stepped out into the hall. The door to the bathroom was open, and I heard the dryer running. I walked in and saw Ephesus leaning over the washer.

"Ephesus! We need to—are you doing my laundry?"

He turned, holding my old prison jumpsuit in his hands. "I needed to wash my clothes, and your stuff was in the way."

He flushed beet red, but in his defense, he had a point. I didn't have that many clothes, but I had somehow managed to scatter *all* of them around the bathroom.

"Well, had I known you were willing to do laundry, I would have been nicer to you on Mars."

"I'm a pretty good baker, too." He coughed and held out his hand. "Where did you get this?"

It was the expired pizza coupon, now even more crumpled than before.

"Just a souvenir from Rott. You can throw it away."

He flattened it and held it up to the light. "Who gave this to you?"

"John and Dowe. Yeah, I know how it sounds."

He jerked his head to face me.

"What? Do you know them?"

He shrugged. "Doesn't everybody know a John Dowe?" He folded the coupon and pocketed it. "Do you want this jumpsuit washed or should I throw it away?"

"As much as I'd like it pressed and mended, we don't have time. There's a problem."

He gave me his full attention.

"Your father just completed Red Rain."

"You're lying," he retorted without hesitation.

"You're right—it's not 100% complete. But he's getting close—give him another few days and he'll be there."

Ephesus's eyes tracked mine.

"He was up late last night working. Now I know why. Whatever Thames said to him yesterday, it must have been convincing."

Satisfied I was telling the truth, Ephesus paled. He opened his mouth, ready to spew a wad of objections and exclamations, then changed his mind. He strode towards the door. "I need to talk to him."

"Save it." I put out my arm and caught him. "We don't have time. We need to get out of here, now."

"Now? Now's like the worst time. It's four o'clock—everyone is still in the building, and it's rush hour out there."

"You want the United to have Red Rain? Because that's what happens if we stay here. Thames is sending a representative at five to review the data."

Ephesus immediately changed gears. "Then our best bet is to make as much disturbance as possible. How big is your bomb?"

"Big enough. We need to wipe the computers—and clear the recycling bin. I don't want them to have any trace of your father's research. I deleted the whiteboard already."

"I'll take care of it." It was said with unequivocal confidence, so I didn't question it. "Get everything ready. I'll meet you in the common room."

He strode out the door without waiting for an affirmative.

I fetched my homemade bomb from its hiding place and ran to the common room. I planted it in the trash can near the door. Then I calibrated the detonator, locked the safety, and put it in my chest pocket.

I went to the vending machine and ordered the most sugary confection I could find. It ended up being these abominable, brightly-colored marshmallow puffs. Even the smell gave me cavities.

While the dispenser was popping them out, I found wire and a battery in the lab to create a makeshift lighter. Then I tipped two of the tables over to form a shield. I used the third table as a stool. I stacked three chairs in a pyramid on top of it and placed the bowl of marshmallows on the seat, putting it as close to the smoke detector as possible.

Smyrna walked in just as I was completing this balancing act. "What are you doing?"

"Preparing a sacrifice to my god."

"Which one?"

"Self-preservation."

Ephesus joined us, a duffle slung over his shoulder. He was cramming several tablets and gadgets from the lab inside. "Nic, where is my flash dri—Dad!"

The old man turned and met eyes with his son. The two wordlessly volleyed emotions back and forth, none of which were pleasant.

I broke it up when I pulled the flash drive out of my pocket and tossed it to Ephesus.

He caught it and, conveniently, didn't question why I had it. He strode to the computer terminal. "Is everything ready?"

I waved the detonator at him.

Smyrna looked between us. "Will someone please tell me what's going on?" he demanded, even though the inflection in his voice indicated he was catching up.

"We're getting out of here," Ephesus cast over his shoulder without looking, "before they realize what you've done."

Smyrna didn't argue. "But how?"

Ephesus plugged the drive into the terminal. He opened the menu and tabbed through the folders. I wondered if he would notice the new additions, but his focused glare never wavered. He found whatever he was looking for and dragged it to the desktop. Then he yanked the drive out, dropped it in his duffle, and zipped it shut. I smiled.

"I need to make a call," he explained, the information directed primarily at me. "If the United eavesdrops on it, they'll know we're up to something. I need you ready to fire as soon as I hang up."

I nodded and held up my homemade lighter.

Understanding flooded Smyrna's eyes with terror. "But what about Phil? If you pull anything, Thames will—"

"You should have thought of her last night if you cared about her safety," Ephesus snarled. He keyed a number into the com app.

"No, you don't understand. Thames said—Ephesus, listen to me." He strode to his son's side and grabbed his arm. Ephesus shrugged him off and hit dial.

The line rang once, twice, three times. "Ephesus, please," Smyrna begged. "Don't do this. I—"

He stopped when the line picked up.

"4th Street Pizza Parlor, how may I help you," a teenage voice droned.

Both Smyrna and I froze.

"Hi, yeah, I'd like to order three house specialties, please. No drinks."

"Carry out or dine in?"

I swore, hopefully loud enough for the kid to hear. "Are you mad?"

Ephesus shushed me. "Do you offer curbside?"

"Sure. Address?"

Ephesus gave it to him.

Smyrna squinted. "Is that…"

Ephesus thanked the kid and hung up. Immediately his hands started flying across the monitor as he opened a program I didn't recognize and typed rapid commands. "Light it up."

"Are you going to tell us what that was all about?" I demanded.

He didn't. "Light it up. Now." The terminal screeched at him.

"Son, are you sure—"

"Do you all want to get out of here alive?" he fairly shouted. "I said, light it up!" He turned to glare at me, his finger posed over a red button on the screen. I couldn't read what it said from this distance.

"Well, I'm about to regret some life choices," I muttered. I ignited the lighter and threw it into the bowl of marshmallows. Instantly the sugar flared into flame.

Ephesus watched the smoke pool along the ceiling. "Dad, get behind the table."

The old man hesitated. I jumped down from the table and demonstrated for him, crouching behind the overturned tables. He reluctantly followed suit.

Ephesus stayed where he was. The minute ticked on, the smoke spreading at the speed of molasses. I was coughing long before the smoke detector kicked in.

Finally, it decided to come to work and erupted with a shriek. I plugged my ears and waited. The smoke thickened. When the detector realized nothing was being done about the situation, the beep changed pitch. Then the sprinklers turned on.

Smyrna flinched and covered his head. Ephesus stayed where he was, even as the water began to run down his face. He was listening.

I filtered past the sirens and spraying water. A fire alarm somewhere else in the building kicked in. Faint shouting. Then, the beep of a door opening, pounding footsteps, and a yelled demand to know "what was going on here."

The door to the common room whooshed open, revealing three guards. Ephesus punched the button on the terminal and shouted, "Now, Nic!"

All three drew their guns. Ephesus dove behind the table. I let the guards take two steps into the room, then released the detonator.

The original plan had been to plant the bomb on the opposite wall. It would provide a distraction, but no one would get blown up in the process.

I altered the plan when I planted the bomb by the door. Those guards definitely wouldn't be chasing after us now.

Smyrna screeched something, but I couldn't filter the words past the ringing in my ears. Ephesus had the dignity to admire the carnage for a split second, then he grabbed his father's arm and hauled him to his feet. "Let's go!"

I followed as he shoved his father through the door to the lab. The old man slipped on the wet tile floor and nearly brought Ephesus down with him. I grasped his other arm and pulled them both out into the hall.

The panel for the main door was beeping erratically, the display flickering on and off like the power was shorting out. "Is that what the emergency protocol is supposed to do?" I shouted at Ephesus.

He shook sopping dark hair out of his eyes. "I don't know!" He waved his hand over the sensor. The panel gave a glitched moan, and the doors slid open halfway.

I pushed the old man out ahead of me. Ephesus squeezed through behind us. Out in the hall, chaos continued to reign. Emergency lights pulsed, and multiple sirens competed for dominance. Every panel on every door was having a similar episode. I was definitely going to have a migraine after this.

"This way!" Ephesus took off down the hall, shoes squishing on the soaked carpet. It wasn't hard to find the exit: Every emergency exit sign was flashing like a fire truck. Ephesus led us to the nearest stairwell, which was packed with businessmen and secretaries fleeing from the upper floors.

Ephesus adjusted the duffle on his shoulder. "All right, act normal and slightly panicked."

"Done," I said.

Smyrna was a bit past the "slightly panicked" stage, but he offered no objection.

Ephesus opened the door, and we merged with the river of people. We flowed as a unit out onto the street, where the rest of the office staff huddled. I struggled to catch snatches of conversation, looking for signs that anyone suspected us.

"What happened?" "Did someone get laid off and pull the fire alarm?" "My makeup is ruined!" "Do you have the time? My phone is locked up." "Is there something wrong with the internet?"

Ephesus followed a group of businessmen headed towards the nearest bus stop. At the curb, a beat-up green sedan idled in a no-parking zone. A teenager with dark hair and antagonistic eyes stood on the sidewalk, holding three pizza boxes.

He glanced down at the receipt. "Three house specials?"

Smyrna gaped. "Stanyard—"

Ephesus gripped his wrist to silence him. "I think you have the wrong address, man. I can give you directions."

"Cool, cool." The kid dropped the pizza boxes in the passenger seat and walked back around to the driver's side.

Ephesus opened the rear door, and we all piled in without a word.

The kid put his blinker on, waiting for a break in traffic. I saw flashing lights in the rearview mirror and opened my mouth to warn him—but it was only a fire truck. It blared its horn, and the kid was all too happy to run a red light to get out of its way.

I waited until we were a few blocks away before glancing back. The scene was a mess, but no one was running after the car waving their arms.

I broke out laughing. Smyrna nearly jumped out of his skin. I patted him consolingly on the shoulder. "I've been waiting months to laugh like that."

Ephesus shot me a look, then leaned towards the front. "Hey, thanks."

The kid gave him a thumbs up. He reached over and flipped one of the pizza boxes open. "Anyone hungry? These are getting cold."

"I am," I said. I leaned forward and grabbed a slice. I nibbled on the rubbery cheese. "Guess John and Dowe weren't kidding about that coupon."

Ephesus grinned and also took a slice.

Smyrna composed himself. "Stanyard? Is that you?"

The kid looked at him in the review mirror. "Hello, Mr. Smyrna." It wasn't said sarcastically.

I cocked an eyebrow at Ephesus. "Friend from camp," he explained.

"Saint Augustine, delivering it hot and fresh." He checked his blind spot, then glanced at me. "So you're Cea's brother."

It was the first time in a long time that I'd been identified by my familial relations—instead of my scientific or criminal achievements—and I didn't know how to respond.

Ephesus made up the difference. "Cea? Is she all right?"

This seemed to snap the old man back to reality. "Philadelphia! Do you know where she is? What have they done with her? Is she safe?" he demanded in rapid succession at a volume much too loud for the close confines of the car.

Stanyard put his hand up. "Hey, calm down, it's okay. They're both fine. They're already at my place."

Smyrna melted into the seat, seeming to lose all his structural integrity. He covered his face with his hands.

Ephesus touched his father's knee. "It's going to be fine. Everything's going to be fine."

I glanced at the duffle at his feet and smiled. "I think you're right."

10

Of all the things I'd contemplated doing to Philadelphia when I found her, hugging was never on the list.

After taking several detours to make sure we weren't being followed, Stanyard drove us to a pizza shop—he was really going all out with this façade—and herded us into a secret basement beneath the building. I was the first down the ladder, and apparently Phil was so elated to see someone in a lab coat that she hugged me without pausing to make a proper identification.

Frankly, she was lucky that my brain was occupied with solving other, more pressing problems. If I'd had more mental energy, I would have prepared a much more appropriate greeting for her.

Not that Ephesus would have let me fulfill my revenge fantasies, but at least I could have gotten a swipe in. The endorphin rush would have been worth it.

For the time being, though, I had to settle for savoring her utter mortification when she realized who she was hugging.

"Glad to see me, Philadelphia? I wish I could say the same of you."

She squeaked. But before I could lord the moment over her, Cea pulled me into the corner and buried me in a hug.

This was a hug I was expecting. But it was no less awkward.

I let her squeeze all of her fear, rage, and aggression out in a rib-bruising embrace. She wasn't making any sound, but I could feel her arms shaking. Once I thought she'd calmed down enough to attempt conversation, I reached up and patted her greasy curls.

"Hey sis."

She sighed in response.

Across the room, the Smyrnas were having a much more verbal reunion. "I'm so glad to see you." "Are you all right?" "What happened?"

"I got knocked out on the way in," Phil confessed.

I glanced over and was mildly gratified to see that she did indeed look like death. "You know they used to say that sleeping after a concussion can kill you."

She gaped at me in horror. Toying with her really was too easy.

"Leave her alone," Ephesus snapped. His muscles tightened in a warning.

I snorted with amusement. "It's just an urban legend. No medical truth to it."

He ignored me and herded his family into the opposite corner where they could pretend to have privacy. Cea tugged on my arm, and I allowed myself to be pulled to the floor next to her, even though I kept my ear tuned to the Smyrnas' conversation.

I turned to look into my sister's eyes for the first time. She was studying me, absorbing me. I waited. I'd learned in childhood that it was more efficient to let Cea talk first.

"You're alive," she said when she was ready.

"Somewhat to my surprise."

"What happened?"

"They sent me to prison," I summarized, not interested in getting graphic. "And when they got tired of banging their heads against the wall trying to make Red Rain work, they fished me out."

"You agreed to give them Red Rain?"

It was impossible to tell how accusatory she was being, but there was definitely more disdain in her voice than I was willing to deflect. "I had absolutely no intention of giving them the formula. You and I both know that I don't possess the knowledge to complete the project, much to my eternal shame."

"So you dragged Ephesus back into it?" Her bitterness was unveiled now. She glanced over her shoulder at him. I followed her gaze.

"Yes," he was saying, also with palpable bitterness, "apparently the United salvaged all my work from Mars and gave it to Dr. Nic to play with."

I answered them both together. "Well, it turned out to be useful, didn't it? We'd have never made it out of there otherwise."

"Never mind," Smyrna inserted, trying and failing to be the parental authority in the room.

Cea returned her glare to me. "You didn't have to get him—them—involved!"

"The United would have had his bombs with or without his person; they had the plans."

I was right, which, as usual, only made her angrier. "Then why'd you do it? Why drag them into this? Why—"

"Because I didn't want to die."

That was the unadulterated truth, which shut her up immediately.

"That's right—I didn't want to die. Is that what I should have done? Bravely volunteered to be executed? Stayed on Rott for the rest of my life? Is that what you want?"

She didn't answer, because there was no answer to that.

I took two slow breaths, counting to ten as I did so. When I spoke again, my voice was soft and brotherly, just how I knew she liked it. "They were going to kill me, Cea, so I thought I'd explore some other options. At least together we had a better chance of escaping."

I added that last bit for her benefit, to help her reconcile her disjointed morals. I knew that if I could help her reach some sort of ethical resolution, we could end the conversation. All she needed was an explanation she could justify, no matter how untrue it was.

I knew that wasn't the reason I had thrown the Smyrnas under the bus. I had no grand designs of becoming allies and staging a brave escape—that was all Ephesus's doing. My plan had simply been to buy myself time. I had every intention of using both of them as scapegoats until I could find a way out.

What I hadn't planned on was the old man completing the formula.

Cea continued to be silent, so I shifted my attention back to the Smyrnas.

"What did you do?" Phil was asking her father. She held his hand and gazed up at him with the purest trust.

She *was* such a stupid little girl.

Smyrna didn't respond. Ephesus did. "*I* worked on hacking the computer and finding an escape route."

His scowl could have set the room on fire.

Phil's peace cracked, and it was beautiful. "Daddy, what happened?"

He weakly squeezed her hand. "I did work on it a little."

"A little?" I yelped, quite involuntarily. "Old man, you nearly had it!"

"Shut *up*," Ephesus snapped, and for once, I thought he might actually follow up on the threat.

The betrayal snuffed the light out of Phil's eyes like a candle. I could see it; I wondered if the old man could. "Daddy, you *worked* on it?"

He met her gaze, but not bravely. "It was the only way. If they didn't see progress, there would have been trouble for all of us."

He wasn't wrong, but Phil was not consoled in the slightest.

"I didn't finish it," he continued. "We couldn't make it work. I highly doubt it will ever be operational."

I opted not to tell them that the near-complete formula was sitting right at their feet, on a flash drive in Ephesus's duffle.

But I wondered what Phil would say if she knew.

63

11

Sleep was a waste of time.

However, I had no intention of sharing my most productive hours with anyone else, so I lay down and pretended to doze, hoping the others would ignore me and follow suit.

Cea lay awake for an annoyingly long time. I knew she was staring at me, but I couldn't tell if it was because she didn't trust me or because she was contemplating the great mysteries of our relationship. Eventually, however, exhaustion did its work, and her breathing settled.

Phil was the next to drop off, although judging by the sweat beading on her forehead, I wondered how long it would last. Her father and brother stayed up talking, evidentially fooled into thinking I was asleep. I watched them through nearly-closed eyelids.

"You lied to her," Ephesus said, too calmly. It was a fact, not an accusation.

The old man was silent.

"About Red Rain," his son continued. "It does work—you almost perfected it. Nic told me."

"I know," was the breathed reply.

"Why did you tell her it would never be operational?"

"She's been through enough." Smyrna reached down and laid his hand on his daughter's shoulder. She flinched in her sleep.

"And it's not over yet. If the government realizes how close you came to finishing it, they'll come after you."

My eyes flung open in the dark. I swore, thankfully not out loud.

The old man responded with a sigh.

"I tried to wipe the computers before we left, but I have no way of knowing what kind of backups they've got going, or how much they saw on the cameras."

"You did your best." Smyrna stiffly patted his son's shoulder. He conveniently didn't mention that he'd already talked to Thames and told the man everything he wanted to know.

Ephesus studied his father, clearly struggling with all the things he probably should be saying. After a painful beat, he deferred with a cowardly, "Let's get some sleep."

Smyrna didn't object. I was grateful. I needed them to drop off so I could get on a computer.

My mind whirled while I waited for them to settle down. Ephesus was right; if Thames truly comprehended how close Smyrna had come, he would hunt him down. And if he caught him, I had no doubt that the old man would complete the formula for him—in exchange for his daughter's life, of course.

If I wanted to be the only one with Red Rain, I had to get away—and I had to take the Smyrnas with me.

The thought gave me absolutely no joy at all, but it was a small price to pay for getting my life back. The question was: Where could we go?

I had an idea, but I needed to do some research. Thankfully, I knew Ephesus had stolen a tablet from the lab.

I waited until I was confident everyone had passed into a deeper state of sleep, then slowly stood up. They'd left the lantern on in the middle of the room, so I had no problems finding Ephesus's duffle. What was problematic, however, was unzipping it without making an obscene amount of noise.

Philadelphia whimpered. I glanced at her, but she was clearly deep into a REM cycle. Her subconscious was torturing her more than I ever could.

I successfully extracted the tablet from the duffle and started up the ladder. I paused beneath the door and listened for Stanyard. I heard what sounded like a TV and a fan running. I pushed on the door gently and was gratified to find that he hadn't replaced the box of junk that had been covering it before.

I lifted the door just enough to look into the room. He was passed out on the bed, fully clothed, in a position that clearly said he hadn't intended to fall asleep. I wondered if some substance had helped him get there.

Between the blaring TV and the creaky fan, there was enough white noise to cover me as I slipped out and closed the door behind me. I quickly climbed the stairs, which were thankfully concrete and didn't squeak, and went out into the garage. I figured I was least likely to be heard—or seen by security cameras—there.

Through the windows in the garage door, I could see that early morning light was already beginning to bleed into the horizon. I sat on a non-greasy patch of concrete and fired up the tablet. I opened the connections menu and found that the shop had public wifi, as all businesses did. The United tried to make it easy for people to connect to the web—one of the perks of allowing the government to spy on all your devices was unlimited data and abundant free hotspots.

It was amazing how many people considered that a fair trade.

I accepted the terms and conditions and logged on. They had no idea who this tablet belonged to—as long as I didn't do anything terribly stupid, I shouldn't raise any red flags.

I opened a browser and pulled up the promotional website for Base #9.6.11.

While the page struggled to load—the signal was a bit weak in the garage—I scolded myself for wishful thinking. Returning to the base on Mars was hugely impractical, if for no other reason than forging interplanetary travel tickets was a nightmare. It could be done, but it would probably cost about the same to buy an abandoned warehouse. If I wanted to set up operations somewhere, I was better off going to the slums or a farm in the middle of the country.

Still, the thought was so deliciously tempting. I had everything I needed—my greatest weapon, plans for numerous bombs and guns, and the scientists who knew how to make it all work. If I could just get back to my castle, I could make it as though the last year never happened.

The page finally loaded, and I was shocked to find that it was untouched.

It was pristine, in fact. All the links worked, and someone had even updated the "current projects" page recently. Most notably, there was absolutely no mention of a government crackdown.

I was still listed as governor. My own poised smile in my staff photo mocked me from the bio page. Myself and I shared a stare as I contemplated the implications. Why wouldn't they take the site down after they'd raided my base? Had they simply been too lazy?

I opened another tab and ran several searches—for the base, for my name, even for Carnegie. There was nothing about the bust anywhere. No news articles, no official statement, no corny propaganda videos.

That was extremely out of character for them. The United loved to make a spectacle out of their conquests. Even the pettiest criminals were burned at the stake to reinforce the government's dominance. The fact that I wasn't mentioned at all was a bit of an insult, really; if I had thwarted a plot to cut an entire *planet* off from the United, I would at least brag about it.

What did they stand to gain by concealing the ordeal?

I kept searching. I tried the Smyrnas. There was no mention of the fictitious transit explosion that had "killed" Ephesus two years ago; according to the public records, he had worked at the same lab on Earth since getting out of college. The only thing available for Phil was her school records.

Smyrna turned up more results—apparently, there'd been a police investigation into his wife's death that had caused a brief flutter of media activity—but his profile had been quiet since then. There was no indication that he'd ever been assigned to Mars.

I tabbed back to the base's website and scrolled through the most recent updates. I suppose, with some mental gymnastics, it wasn't too hard to justify keeping Project 74 a secret. After all, the United had decided to simply pick up where I'd left off and create Red Rain for themselves. It made sense that they wouldn't want to advertise their new superweapon before it was complete.

But why leave the base's site up? Why was there no mention of Smyrna going to Mars? Those records should have been public. And what about Ephesus's transit explosion? That absolutely should have made the news. Either the explosion had never gotten reported, or someone had made the effort to go back and scrub the data after Ephesus returned from the dead. Both options raised a litany of insidious questions.

A thought pecked at the edge of my consciousness. If all the public records were untouched, some other things might be intact, too—like my login to the base's website. I was sure they'd been smart enough to change my access codes to the sensitive databases, but the base's blog might have slipped under their radar.

I navigated to the login. The site accepted my username and then prompted me to use face ID. I held the tablet up to my face, wondering if it would work in the half-light of the garage.

It did. The circle flashed green and the control panel loaded—at the same time the door behind me slammed.

"What are you doing?"

I glared over my shoulder, annoyed. Stanyard stood on the step. "Where did you get that tablet?"

"It's fine," I dismissed him, turning back to my work.

He was upon me in two steps and leering over my shoulder. "What site is that?" He rudely snatched the tablet from my hands without allowing me the dignity of answering. He scanned the screen, anger and fear burning the grogginess out of his eyes. "You hacked into the base's website?" His voice shot up an octave.

"I didn't have to hack in."

He wasn't interested in the technicalities. "And on the public wifi? You idiot!" he screamed, followed by a few more colorful words. He threw the tablet at me. I missed, and it landed on the concrete with a crack. "They're going to trace this."

I picked the tablet up and brushed off the damaged screen. "I doubt anyone's spying on the internet usage from your rat-infested pizza parlor."

"Are you deaf?" He was yelling like I was. "You literally just blew up their lab yesterday—you don't think they're watching for any activity on your accounts? Someone's definitely going to see this and trace the device back to here."

He looked like he was contemplating punching me, then wisely thought better of it. He sighed and pinched the bridge of his nose. "We need to get you out of here, now."

"If you're so worried, I'll take the tablet to the coffee shop down the road and log in again. Then they'll think I've moved on."

He wagged his head. "And let you out of my sight? Too risky."

I shrugged. "It's your funeral."

Stanyard spun on his heel and raced out of the garage. I stood up and went back to the browser, only to find that half the screen was pixelated, thanks to the kid's rage. I sighed and turned the device off.

To his credit, the kid was prepared to move. Within five minutes he had everyone awake and in the garage ready to leave.

Cea slapped me before I could even make eye contact. In retrospect, I probably should have been prepared for that.

"What were you thinking?" she hissed in a whisper that was just the right pitch to make my ears ring.

"I was phoning home," I replied, rubbing my cheek.

As usual, she wasn't listening and forged ahead. "You're going to get us all killed! Why are you always so—"

"Hey." Ephesus shoved himself between us. "Save it for when you don't have to whisper."

Cea snarled, but she obeyed on the first try—a luxury she had never afforded me. I studied Ephesus and reached the somewhat uncomfortable conclusion that he had been "busy" with more than one project over the past few months.

The door slammed, and Stanyard returned. "Everyone in. Who's volunteering to ride in the trunk?" The hatch on his dying green sedan popped open with a weak chirp.

"Nic and I will," Cea said with a glare that told me not to object, not that I had any intention of wasting energy on something as pedestrian as seating arrangements.

The others started clambering into the car. Cea slid into the trunk with an agility that was leftover from her cheerleading days. I waited until she had arranged herself, then climbed in after her. I briefly considered facing away from her, but thought better of it.

With some maneuvering of my long legs, we fit. Our knees were pressed together and our foreheads were nearly touching. One of her bedraggled curls tickled my nose. It reminded me of all the times we had hidden under the bed or buried ourselves in blanket forts as children. Her curls had been much longer then. I would have made a comment about it had I thought she was in the mood for reminiscing.

Stanyard slammed the hatch without ceremony, plunging us into stuffy darkness.

I thought Cea would use the privacy to resume her tirade, but she didn't. She was silent, her breathing eerily steady.

The car groaned to life. I hoped our commute would be short, or the vibrating of the engine would give me a migraine in short order.

The car eased down the driveway and idled at the street for a long moment—long enough that I ventured conversation. "There's no record of my arrest in the news," I declared.

"I know," she replied, voice so soft that it was difficult to hear her over the engine. Muffled chatter came from up front, and the car turned onto the road.

Clearly she had been watching my file while I was gone. "Don't you think that's odd?"

"Yeah, I—"

Her sentence was lost to the successive sounds of a gun firing, glass shattering, and Philadelphia screaming. I knew it was her; I'd heard that sniveling scream more times than I cared to count.

Cea swore. I did the same as the unwelcome realization dawned on me that I was wrong.

Stanyard had been right. They had been watching my accounts.

Very closely, apparently.

The car swerved, and then the engine revved for all it was worth—which sadly wasn't much. I tried to mentally calculate the odds of our escape, but judging by the laboring of the engine, we were starting at a disadvantage.

"They must really want you!" Cea shrieked. It wasn't accusatory.

The car jerked around a corner. I grunted as my head bounced against the roof of the trunk. *I hope this kid knows how to drive!*

"I think it's the base!" I shouted to be heard. My neurons continued to fire even as I struggled to maintain some sense of direction. "Something's going on—there's no reason why—"

My eardrums shattered as a bullet ripped into the trunk and Cea yelled.

"Laodicea!" I reached for her, just as the car took another hairpin turn and slammed me against the side.

"Nic," she wailed, voice shaky.

I scrambled towards her. I grasped her shoulder and felt blood. "Cea…"

And then we crashed.

The car whipped around and slammed into something solid. All the forward motion ricocheted back into the truck, hurling both Cea and me against the wall.

The wind left me like birds scared out of a thicket. Pain throbbed against my temples, as if the leftover inertia was still trying to escape. I forced myself to take even breaths, counting off the seconds between each inhale and exhale, even as I reached over and felt for Cea.

"Cea?"

She was silent.

"Cea!" I rolled over and found her neck. A quick examination told me both her breathing and pulse were steady; she had simply been knocked unconscious.

I gingerly felt the wound on her shoulder. It was superficial; the bullet must have just grazed her.

The trunk popped open. Instantly I was assaulted with sunlight, sirens, and the delirious shouting of the others.

I sat up and looked at Cea. She appeared to be sleeping, her angelic curls cast around her head. She was slightly pale, but I knew she'd be fine.

I clambered out of the car and scanned the area. We'd crashed into a dumpster behind a warehouse. There were two exits—we could go back to the street, where the cop cars were rapidly approaching, or we could cut down the alley and maybe lose them in the inner city.

It was feasible. I knew I could make it.

Smyrna. I whipped around. I couldn't see Phil, but the old man was bent over the passenger seat. "Smyrna!" I yelled. "This way!"

He didn't hear me. I ran to him and caught his arm. "Old man, we have to move, *now!*"

He shrugged me off; my hand left a smear of blood on his soiled lab coat. "If you want to be useful, go get help!"

"What?" I didn't understand what I was hearing, but I didn't have time to argue. I had to get him out of here. If the United caught him, it would all be over.

I grabbed his shoulders and dragged him back, betting on the fact that I was younger and stronger than him. He resisted. "Thomas, for the love of God, let's go!"

He whipped around and shoved me. It was a reaction I'd never expected from him, and I was woefully unprepared. I stumbled backward into the car.

"Don't you get it?" he panted. "I'm not going anywhere!"

"You fool—" I started, but then I glanced past him and saw Ephesus slumped over the passenger seat, face bloodied beyond recognition.

And that's when I acknowledged that I'd lost.

Smyrna would never make it. Or, more accurately, he would *refuse* to make it.

I saw flashing lights approaching out of my peripheral. I became aware of Stanyard screaming at Phil to *come on.*

I didn't move. I knew there was no point in running or panicking. I looked down at my hand and rubbed Cea's blood between my fingers.

The United had what they came for.

12

Of course I was sentenced to Rott. It was the obvious choice, and the United was, above all, predictably obvious. It was one of her worst traits.

What annoyed me was that it took them an idiotically long time to do it. Wasting three perfectly good days in solitary confinement just to be told something I already knew was an insult.

Perhaps that was their intent. If so, they were succeeding with an uncharacteristic amount of efficiency.

I suspected, however, that the delay had little to do with me. In fact, I spent the better part of those three days resigning myself to the uncomfortable reality that what happened from here on out would have next to nothing to do with me.

I had outlived my usefulness to the United. I had known that months ago, but their small minds were finally coming to terms with the prospect. Smyrna was now their primary target.

I found this new reality bothersome, but not because I minded deferring the stage to greater men. Of course it was irksome that the old man had been able to solve in a weekend what had eluded me for years, but I knew how to set aside my pride in favor of results. What perturbed me was the realization that I would now be an accessory to his life's story. I had become the accomplice, the witness, the bystander.

There was no thought more loathsome. If I was going to suffer in prison, I demanded to be the cause of my own calamity.

I correctly assumed that I was being made to wait while the bureaucracy ran Smyrna through the wringer. They were probably interrogating him right now, trying to threaten or bribe him into finishing his work.

How I longed to be in their shoes. Every fiber of my being wished it were my fingers around his daughter's throat, making him dance for me. I had been right, right about everything. Red Rain could work, and Smyrna was the man to do it.

If only I had realized how close I had been to perfection back when we were on Mars. If I had known I held the key to success in my hands, if I hadn't underestimated that brat of a girl, I could have had everything I wanted.

That was my mistake. I had underestimated them, all of them. I'd underestimated Ephesus. I'd underestimated Smyrna. And I'd let a stupid teenager in a skirt upstage me.

She had hovered in my blind spot the whole time. Why? Why had I overlooked her? Why had I underestimated her determination to live?

I knew the answer, however much I tried to conceal it with circumstantial evidence: It was because she was a Christian. I had assumed that anyone who allowed themselves to be detained in a camp was weak and unprincipled. I had expected her to buckle under pressure. I had expected her to compromise. I had expected her to be like my sister.

My own prejudice had ruined me, and I couldn't deny it. I had finally fulfilled that Proverb Cea liked to quote at me: "Pride comes before a fall." Even broken clocks are right twice a day, and this was clearly not my hour.

My suspicions were confirmed when, after three days of boredom, they stuffed me in a car with Ambrose and Phil. If I were them, I would have kept Phil close at hand, in case her father needed additional incentive, but to each his own.

I was not the least bit surprised that they sent Ambrose with us. I knew Ambrose had also outlived his usefulness, but he hadn't figured that out yet.

I spent the first part of the ride to the docks savoring the taste of the pure, well-aged hatred I had for both of them. But after a few minutes, I came to the conclusion that having feelings was a waste of energy. Ambrose was inconsequential; eventually he would take himself out with his own stupidity. Phil was annoying, but even I had to admit that my misfortune wasn't her fault. I was the one who hadn't watched my back.

As soon as our ship launched and Ambrose got bored with supervising us, I put as much distance between myself and both of them as possible. I correctly assumed that Phil would have zero desire to be crammed in the hold with a bunch of men, so that's where I intended to wait out the voyage.

I waded into the crowd, embracing the anonymity while it lasted. On Rott there would be too many people that knew me, too many people who wanted to call me either friend or enemy. There would be no rest for the wicked on Rott.

The next day, I begrudgingly surfaced for first meal. The rations could barely be considered food, but, unlike a certain someone who was noticeably absent from the line, I knew that refusing to eat only put me at a disadvantage.

Out of boredom I decided to take a lap around the deck. Might as well get a head start on my steps before we landed. That was when I saw the fight.

I'll never tell Phil that I saw the whole thing. She'll never know that I could have stopped Ambrose from tossing her reader overboard had I intervened a moment earlier. I'll keep that information to myself, although if she ever annoys me enough, I might let it slip.

I watched the whole exchange from a comfortable distance. They were both too absorbed in their emotions to notice me—

Phil in her pathetic capitulations and Ambrose in his even more pathetic power trip.

I smiled when Phil punched Ambrose. It was impressive, and the shock on his face was the most entertaining thing I'd seen in weeks.

My smile faded when he punched her back.

At first, I was jealous. How many times had I longed to slap her, hit her, even kill her? It was infuriating to watch Ambrose, who was a sniveling coward of a man, do what I'd been too polite to do myself.

But when he kicked her—one, two, three times—a different emotion came over me. I thought of Cea and remembered why, against my better judgment, I had always been too kind to the Smyrnas.

"Hey!"

Ambrose stopped mid-strike to look at me.

"I'm curious: Did the United train you to hit women, or are you just that vile on your own?"

I could tell by the looks on their faces that neither of them knew what to make of that, and I loved it. I slathered on the sarcasm. "I'll admit to being a little impressed, though. I mean, you had the guts to hit a woman in front of all these men, whose protective instincts might flare up at any moment. Even I don't have the courage to do that."

Ambrose laughed, and it gave me an immense amount of pleasure to cut it off with a punch to his gut.

The resulting scuffle—I wouldn't gratify it by calling it a "fight"—was immensely therapeutic. Why hadn't I thought to start something before? This was genius. Each punch I landed released a little bit of tension, and watching the growing frustration on his face was downright delicious. He did get a few weak slaps in, but they only gave me more adrenaline.

I was so high on the drug that I forgot Phil was even there. She screamed when Ambrose caught me off-guard and knocked me back on the deck. Did she actually think I was going to get hurt? How quaint.

I was a little disappointed when the captain interrupted us. I would have loved to continue the jaunt a little longer, but all good things must come to an end.

"What is the meaning of this?" he demanded.

Even though I thought the situation was rather obvious, I decided to help him out. "Just having a friendly duel in defense of a lady. All in the good fun."

I watched the captain read the room and reach the appropriate conclusions. All I had to do was stand back and grin as he sent Ambrose to timeout and put Phil away where she wouldn't cause trouble.

Phil was a bit slow on the draw. As usual, she idiotically assumed she was in trouble. But as they lead her away, she seemed to connect the dots.

She glanced over her shoulder at me. I could tell she was crunching the numbers, trying to gauge how much goodness had been behind my actions.

Don't think too hard. You might strain a muscle.

I'm not sure what conclusion she reached—I didn't care. But she did mouth a "thank you."

I acknowledged it with a nod.

13

Tower wasn't surprised to see me back on Rott.

He seemed—well, his expression was ambiguous at best. He greeted me with a raised eyebrow, peering down from his rusty patrol perch. But that gesture could have meant anything— amusement, confusion, speculation.

But at least it wasn't disdain. There hadn't been a trial on the mainland, a somewhat unexpected mercy. But what the United had lacked in legal process, I was confident my familiars on Rott would more than make up with public scrutiny.

And if there was one thing I couldn't stand, it was judgment from lesser men. Most of the prisoners on Rott had been put away for petty crimes—theft, propaganda, smuggling. At least I had *attempted* an act of insurrection. Most of these men had no idea what it meant to truly buck the system. Most had never tried. They could never understand me.

I could only hope they would all quickly tire of the spectacle of my arrival and return to the comfort of their monotonous lives.

They put me back in my old cell, which was either an attempt at irony or sheer laziness. Judging by the way the dust had settled on the desk and bed sheets, it didn't look like the room had been occupied since I'd left.

Perhaps they had known I would need it again.

As usual, however, the locked door didn't afford me any privacy. Not ten minutes after I'd been deposited in my cell, Ambrose came knocking.

I looked up to see him eagerly sliding his hands up and down the bars of the window. He had clearly been planning this moment for a very long time, so I let him play out his fantasy, hoping it would end more quickly if I didn't interrupt.

He savored the moment until he got bored, which thankfully was only about thirty seconds. "Well, let's be going," he said, as if we'd both known this was coming all along.

Perhaps, in a way, we both did.

I followed him down a floor, where we picked up Phil. She looked annoyed but wisely said nothing.

Ambrose unhelpfully filled the silence. "I'm here to assign you to your new jobs."

They were finally going to rectify my unemployment. Being put to work might be considered an act of mercy, although I'm sure Ambrose would do everything in his power to turn it into cruel and unusual punishment.

We followed him to the factory at the center of the island. It looked like construction had been completed; all the scaffolding and building debris had been swept away, and steam churned steadily from the smokestacks into the sky. A deep rumble could be heard vibrating through the walls.

That rumble grew as we descended an elevator three floors down. The doors opened, dumping us onto a platform that overlooked a cavernous factory. It must have been at least the size of a football field, crammed to the overflowing with machines that were laboring like they were late to work.

I think, subconsciously, I knew what it was as soon as I saw it. Something about the smell, the sound, the sight of the three-story-tall storage silos at the far end of the room—I had seen it all before. In dreams, in concept sketches, in crude diagrams scribbled on the whiteboard during late-night planning sessions with Carnegie. This was my factory.

But still, I had to ask. "What is this factory making?"

He sneered, which was enough answer for me, but he had the gumption to use words anyway. "We're making Red Rain."

Phil had the decency to express the expected human emotions of horror, grief, and fear. Me, I couldn't muster up the energy to be surprised. It was inevitable. The only surprising thing was that I hadn't seen it before; my only regret was that I had made it all possible.

"Wow," I murmured, feeling the need to acknowledge my role. "I guess the old man really did have it."

Phil was livid. She threw a decent fit, insisting that they couldn't make her do this and that she'd rather die than produce an ounce of the abominable liquid.

I left Ambrose to sort out that problem. I walked up to the railing and took it all in. In spite of myself, I couldn't turn off my engineer's brain. As I scanned the factory, I mentally calculated how it all worked, traced the product flow, and estimated the output. It was a decently constructed factory. I would have made a few changes to increase efficiency, but it would suffice to win a war, no doubt.

Not that there would be any more wars after the United revealed their weapon.

I tried to explain this concept to Phil over dinner, but she wasn't having it. She'd been assigned to do literally pointless paperwork in Ambrose's office, so we hadn't seen each other since morning. I'd been sent to monitor the control panels on the side of the storage silos—a job that was only slightly less useless.

I had hoped a day of slaving as Ambrose's secretary would cool her down, but apparently I'd misjudged her yet again. If anything, she was even more fired up. She sought me out across the mess hall and, before even taking a bite, launched into a spiel about how we had to stop production.

"It's too late," I insisted, hoping to let her down quickly.

"No, it's not. They can't have had that factory operational for more than a few days. There's no way they've already shipped a boatload back to the mainland."

"Not that…" I sighed. I was far too exhausted to be engaging in this kind of moral debate. How do you explain to an optimist that the game is over? "I mean it's too late—just, how do you propose destroying something that eats metal?"

"Why are you eating metal for lunch? The rations aren't *that* bad, except on pizza day."

I looked up to see John and Dowe approaching our table and realized my night was about to get much worse.

They collectively ogled Phil. "Oh, you brought a lady friend back with you! How nice!"

"Dowe, she's too young for him. Don't be disgusting."

"You're right. She could definitely do better, John."

It was almost enough to make me believe in either God or the devil. Clearly, one of them had sent these two to torture me before my time.

Phil glanced rapidly between them, going cross-eyed. "You're John… and Dowe?" She looked back at me.

I shook my head. She was on her own with these two. "And you thought 'Tower' was a weird name."

"So how you doing, Q? I didn't expect you back so soon." John and Dowe confirmed my worst fears and sat down at the table with us.

I looked them dead in the eyes. "But you did expect me back."

They shrugged and started eating.

Phil was still studying the pair. "Are you… friends?"

I sighed. "What did I tell you about friends?"

"Whatever he told you was wrong!" Dowe jostled the table with an emphatic thump. "We are definitely your friends, so don't listen to this stick-in-the-mud."

"Yeah! We're way more fun than he is, anyway."

Well, aren't you three going to get on like a house on fire?

Phil looked to me. "Should I tell… them?"

Tell them what? I wanted to snap, but I knew. I also knew I didn't have to put up with this basal conversation. I started gathering my trash. "Pretty sure we're not the only people on the island who know what that factory is making," I droned, and then stood up and left the table.

She watched me leave. I hoped she got the message. I didn't know how to make it more obvious, short of yelling "shut up and leave me alone" to her face. I wasn't interested in her revolution.

We had lost. My greatest enemy had my life's work, all because I was a coward. I'd called on the Smyrnas to save my own skin, and the United had gotten everything they wanted. They won and would continue to win with the help of my weapon. No amount of kicking against the bars of my cage would change that.

I could only hope Phil would take the hint.

14

Phil did take the hint, at least for twenty-four hours.

John and Dowe, however, did not.

"Hey Q, you awake?" they hissed through the door of my cell at an hour when I definitely should have been.

I put the pillow over my face. "You know I can't sleep without a bedtime story."

"Well, have we got a story for you!" They snickered, and then the door to my cell popped open with a chirp.

I jerked upright. "What the—"

They sauntered in, both unashamedly clothed in pajamas. "Slumber party!"

I was too dumbstruck to object as they crammed themselves onto my tiny cot. "How did you—"

"Oh that?" John gestured his shoulder at the door. "Just a little thing I whipped up called a master key…"

I glared at him. I wasn't sure which would be more loathsome—him joking about having a master key, or him not telling me he had one.

"Actually," Dowe said, mercifully sparing me any further sarcasm, "the door wasn't locked."

"I'm sorry?"

"Tower did us a solid. The lock on your door is conveniently 'malfunctioning.' It hasn't been locked all night. You didn't notice?"

I stared at the open door. "Never thought to try." It wasn't like I had anywhere to go.

"And that," Dowe jabbed me in the shoulder, "is exactly your problem, Q. You don't try."

"First step to self-improvement is acknowledging the problem. Step one, check!"

"Spare me step two." I contemplated kicking them off the bed but wasn't sure I wanted that much physical contact.

John had no such qualms. He planted both hands on my shoulders and shoved me off my own bed. I was so startled and disgusted that I made a yelping sound I am not proud of.

I stumbled to my feet and whipped around. "Get out!"

They were both oblivious and settled in to fill the vacuum of space I had left. "The second step," John continued seamlessly, tucking my blanket over his knees, "is to get off your butt and change things."

I sighed. "You're right, there is something I need to change— my room number."

John cackled like he actually thought that was funny.

Dowe attempted to hold me in his gaze. "What happened, Q?"

Of course I knew what he was generally referring to, but the question was too vague to gratify it with a functional answer. "I lost a bet."

"No, you didn't." Dowe spoke quietly, more quietly than I'd ever heard either of them speak. "We did."

For the first time since we'd met, he stared at me with clear eyes full of intelligence. "We took a gamble on you, Q."

I returned his stare, feeling absolutely no remorse. "That was your first mistake."

"And now the entire free world has to pay out." Dowe gestured in the general direction of the factory. "We could have bailed you out, Q. All you had to do was order pizza."

"Unfortunately, the kid doesn't offer a gluten-free option."

John gagged.

Dowe wasn't fooled. "Why did you tell them about Smyrna?"

I had no desire to confess my sins to him like I'd done with Cea. "The United would have gone to Smyrna as soon as they figured out I couldn't do it—I didn't have to tell them anything."

It was a plausible explanation, but I didn't truly believe it. If the United had realized Smyrna was their man, they would have tried him first. But according to the paper trail I left on Mars, Smyrna hadn't been involved in the project at all; I hadn't even granted him full access to Wing 74 yet. Only Carnegie and I had known how qualified the old man really was.

No, I was fully aware that, had I not said anything, the Smyrnas might have slipped under the United's radar. In spite of myself, I was beginning to profoundly regret dragging the old man into it—but not for the reasons Dowe was expecting.

John, with a spurt of wisdom not belied by his facial expression, said, "Well, no use crying over spilled milk. How do we fix it?"

I rubbed the bridge of my nose. "You don't."

"I said 'we.'"

"I know, and I don't care."

"We've got, at best, a few days before they ship a load back to the mainland. We need to blow up that factory, and fast," Dowe inserted.

"Oh, you want to blow it up? Luckily for you, I know just the woman for the job. And she lives on *another floor*." I stood back and jabbed my finger at the door.

John frowned. "Phil ain't always going to be around to clean up your messes, Q."

I had no patience to dissect the moral implications of that statement, if any were intended. "We're done here."

"You're the only one who can end this, Nic."

If Dowe was hoping to foster an emotional connection by using my real name, he failed. "I just did. Leave."

"Nah." John flopped back on the pillow. "We've got all night."

I growled, my frustration reaching the boiling point. I considered using a loud volume and swift fists to make my point, but instead I opted to be as clear and precise as possible in hopes of avoiding any ambiguity. I dumbed my voice down to a five-year-old level and stated, "Get out. Leave me alone. I'm not interested in your war for independence, and I won't help you."

"That's no way to talk to your friends, Q," Dowe scolded.

"We're trying to help!"

"I don't need your help." I met their eyes. "And we're not friends."

Somewhat to my disappointment, neither man looked offended by the latter statement. "That's debatable," Dowe said with a raised eyebrow. He didn't clarify what he meant.

Thankfully, I didn't care. "Get out," I repeated, hoping the third time was the charm. "And tell Tower that he'd better get my door lock 'fixed,' or I'll report the oversight to his superiors."

John blew a raspberry. "Tell him yourself." He jumped up and sauntered out the door.

Dowe followed at a calmer pace. He paused in the doorway and glanced back.

I eyed him. "Don't."

He shrugged. "I was just gonna say—I hope you got a good seat in the peanut gallery."

"Excuse me?"

He didn't elaborate. "Just don't bring any *actual* peanuts—I'm allergic."

And with that, he left and closed the door behind him.

A few minutes later, I heard the deadbolt slide shut.

15

The worst part about my prison job was that there wasn't any actual work involved.

The entirety of my job description was to sit and watch the machines work. I monitored the controls on the side of the holding tanks, mindlessly observing while the dials and digits cataloged the ongoing production. I hadn't even been given instructions on what each display meant or what to do in case of a malfunction. I was literally supposed to just watch.

Ambrose was probably hoping it would be torturous for me to watch someone else produce my weapon, but he underestimated the totality of my resignation to failure. He also forgot that I had three PhDs; within six hours I had completely worked out how the factory operated and sketched a flow chart in my mind. I also figured out there were thirty-seven dials, buttons, and switches across the factory that I could access without any security clearance—four of which were on the holding tanks.

None of this information was in any way useful. I could have easily jammed the system and made a big mess, and I thought about doing it, just for the amusement. But causing any long-term damage to the factory would require computer access, which was something they wisely hadn't given me.

Still, mapping out the flow of the factory distracted me long enough to get me through my shift. What I was going to do tomorrow, or the day after, I had no idea, but at least I'd survived one day without my brain withering from atrophy.

Phil watched me the entire shift. I knew because every time I glanced towards the control booth, I saw her looking down at me. I could tell she hadn't given up the fight yet; her face was permanently glued into a concentrated frown, and she paced the office like a caged rabbit. I could also tell she was silently judging me, weighing whether or not she should involve me in whatever pathetic revolution she was cooking up. I desperately hoped she would decide I wasn't worth the effort.

No such luck. I knew I was in for it when she hung back in the elevator at the end of our shift.

"Meet me at Tower's place after dinner," she hissed.

I sighed loudly, but she was already scampering away, attempting to look natural.

She avoided me for the entire meal, as if that would defer suspicion. Someone probably should have told her that it was actually *more* suspicious than not, but I certainly wasn't going to volunteer the information.

John and Dowe also spared me the misery of their company. I didn't see them at all, in fact, or anyone I knew. Everyone at the nearby tables completely ignored me. I was able to eat in undisturbed peace and solitude, just like I'd always wanted.

I hope you got a good seat in the peanut gallery.

I rolled Dowe's words around in my head as I chased the last bite of gruel around the bottom of my bowl.

Then, with a dramatic grunt that was appreciated by no one at the tables around me, I slammed my spoon down and went to find Tower.

He watched me approach from across the yard. When I got closer, he gave a jerk of his head towards the shadows behind his post. Phil was there, overtly fidgeting.

Her face brightened when she saw me. *Don't get too excited, buttercup.*

She didn't wait for me to say anything and launched right into her spiel. "We need to destroy Red Rain."

I raised one eyebrow.

"I have to try. I won't just stand by and watch while they destroy the world. I can't…"

She paused. I waited.

She took a deep breath of resolve. "*We* can't let them do that."

Why did everyone think I was going to fall for that? "Why don't you just destroy it yourself? You've done it once before."

Her eyes flickered, but she kept her cool. "There aren't any tables of chemicals I can turn over. And I need your help."

For once, her voice carried a palpable amount of sarcasm. She was finally speaking my language, so I took the bait. "Why do you need my help?"

"Because I'm no good with computers," she declared humbly, as if I didn't already know that.

"You seem to do just fine hacking security systems."

"Only because I stole a device *you* invented."

"I'm impressed that you'll admit to stealing."

"We need to hack the computer in Ambrose's control room." Much to my disappointment, she dropped the sass and got back to practicality. And I had just come up with a great comeback. "From there we can wipe their data and shut down the operation."

It wasn't the worst plan—at least, it was a better plan than I would have expected from her. Regrettably, however, that wasn't how computers worked, and her naivety fell short of being adorable. "Even if… even *after* I hack into the computer, it will be incredibly difficult to erase the data such that it's irretrievable. It is almost impossible to permanently delete information from a computer."

"I know. But this will do it for you." She reached into her pocket and withdrew Ephesus's flash drive.

I hoped my surprise didn't color my facial expression. I was impressed; Ephesus had been smart enough to split his work up, and Phil had been smart enough to hide the drive. But while I'm sure Ephesus had downloaded some intriguing files, there was also something else very important stored on that drive.

I decided to tell her, just to see how she'd react. "What good will that do? That has all the Red Rain files on it too, you know."

"What?"

She sounded like she'd been slapped, and I mildly enjoyed it. "I transferred the complete research files from the lab before we escaped. I'm sure the United added a bit after we left, but I could easily figure it out from your father's notes."

She washed pure white. I decided to have some mercy and keep the conversation on track. "But how is that going to help us destroy their operation?"

Her fingers clenched around the drive. "It also contains my brother's virus."

With a flash of recognition, everything snapped into place. That's why Ephesus had been so confident he could wipe the computers at the lab. That was the mysterious program he'd run right before we broke out—he'd unleashed his data virus.

It was a virus designed to wipe all data from all devices it infected. It was also the one I had prematurely released onto the internet because I was too inept to realize the system wasn't fully secure. Through some bizarre miracle, the virus hadn't been fully functional then—Ephesus had sabotaged it. But now—

"Yes," Phil said slowly, her eyes tracking mine. "He and Cea fixed it."

The mention of Ephesus and my sister in the same sentence caused uncategorizable emotions to flare. "So the little twerp *did* know how to code it properly."

Phil's nose twitched disdainfully. "Yes, and if you upload it to the computer in the control room, it will completely wipe their systems."

The silence stretched for a beat, but not because I didn't have anything to say. No, my brain was firing rapidly, fueled by the somewhat disconcerting realization that the virus changed everything.

Phil tested the waters. "Hopefully it's a closed system so nothing else will be affected."

I shook my head. "Yes, no doubt it's a very secured private system, but if we're lucky the gates won't be too hard to crack. They must have some way they're transmitting progress reports back to the mainland. If we can find out how, hopefully we can use that access to open a two-way door."

I looked up and realized she wasn't getting it. "Wiping the control system in the factory won't be enough. The United will have copies of the research on their mainland computers. Even if we destroy the factory, they can rebuild it. If we want to stop them from producing Red Rain, we need to wipe all their systems."

As I talked it out, the implications took root in my stomach. Playing with the virus was an insane gamble, but it was a bet I was willing to take. If I could pull this off, I could still keep Red Rain out of the hands of my greatest enemy.

And I'd put anything on the line for a chance to do that.

"If we're going to do this, we have to do it right. We need to hack through the computer and upload the virus to the internet, wiping everything. We have to erase Red Rain from their systems for good!"

I hadn't realized I'd raised my voice until Tower shushed me from above. I took a deep breath and locked eyes with Phil, hoping I was getting through to her. "We have to use the virus as it was originally intended."

"But that will erase everything!" she squeaked in terror. "The Bibles—"

I groaned. *That's what you're worried about? You'd trade an ancient book for the known free world?* "Then why did your brother create the virus? He didn't have to rewrite it. Why would he code it and keep it on hand, if it wasn't for a situation like this? We have to use it."

I reached for the drive. She pulled her hand back.

I grunted and weighed my options. It would not be that hard to force the drive from her hand. Even Tower probably wouldn't stop me, if he'd been listening to our conversation.

But while I could probably accomplish this act of rebellion on my own, it would be a lot easier with a second set of hands.

I looked up into her face. And I waited.

She eyed me—judging me, weighing me. I let her.

After a moment, she held the drive out.

I nodded in recognition, then went back to business. "This still won't be enough. We have to destroy the product they've already made."

"Why?"

"For one, there's enough in there already to desecrate a small country. I did the calculations during my shift today. And two, there's a risk they can reconstruct the formula from a completed sample. We have to destroy their reserves so there's no trace left."

"How are we supposed to destroy something that can eat metal?" She threw my own words back at me; had I been in a different mood, I might have appreciated the irony.

As it was, I ignored her and mentally retraced the plans I had sketched of the factory. I followed the flow of chemicals, snatching at every dial, crank, and access point we could potentially manipulate. I calculated a dozen ways to jam the machines, but disposing of the completed product was problematic. Releasing a warehouse worth of condensable gas right next to an ocean seemed ill-fated. Even a wave of wet sea breeze could cause it to liquify and—

I blinked. "We let it burn."

"What?"

I threaded my words carefully. "We drain the vats. If we can release the acid and get it to condense, Red Rain will burn through the floor and destroy itself."

It was pure poetry. We paid it a moment of respectful silence.

"We'll need to get Ambrose out of the factory during working hours when all the systems are open and online," I continued, mentally checking off all the potential hiccups to my idea.

"How?"

How indeed? Before my analytical brain could process that problem, an inhumanly cheerful voice joined the conversation. "How about a distraction?"

John and Dowe appeared beside us. By the way they casually stepped out of the shadows, I could tell they had been standing nearby for a decent amount of time. "Tower!" I glared up at him.

He didn't gratify me with eye contact. "I didn't think they were a problem."

John repeated himself. "How about a distraction?"

"A big one," Dowe echoed.

"We could do a demonstration!"

"Those are always fun!"

"We could make it like a talent show, and Philli here can help us. I bet she can put on a real good distraction!"

In his defense, that *was* one of her better talents.

Dowe flicked him in the ear. "Don't be a fool! We don't want a woman getting tangled up in a demonstration. This could get messy."

The gears started turning, and suddenly I realized that Tower might not be wrong about these two.

"We need it to be messy," I said, stepping closer. "Really messy. 'All guards on deck' messy."

I glanced between them, hoping the expression on my face was encouraging. It wasn't an emotion I practiced very often.

My efforts were rewarded with identical grins.

In an attempt to secure our alliance, I did something I'd never dreamed I'd do: I smiled back.

Dowe winked.

"Oh, I think we and a couple dozen of our prison buddies can handle that," John sneered.

"Let's ask Art."

"And Marty. And that guy who calls himself 24... What's his real name again?"

"I think it's Cloud."

"How's that a real name? You sure the guy ain't duping us with a double-double alias?"

Phil and I collectively ignored them. "Commander Ambrose always locks the control room door when he leaves," she said. "What if he takes the time to lock it this time?"

As if locked doors had ever stopped her. "If that happens, you can figure out a way to circumvent the lock."

She wisely did not argue. "When should we do it?"

"Tomorrow." Tower's head emerged from his window. "A ship is coming at noon to transport the first batch of Red Rain. If you want to keep the reserves out of the hands of the United, you need to destroy it before that ship comes."

The implications backhanded me. "Tomorrow is my floor's 'day off,'" I groaned. "We're all forcibly confined to our quarters. For lack of a better phrase, I'll be locked in my room."

Unless the lock on my door were to conveniently "malfunction."

Tower and Phil shared a long look. She silently pleaded with him. He studied her—looking for what, I'll never know.

Then his gaze shifted to me.

Your move, friend.

He broke eye contact and retracted into his tower. "I'll make it happen." And then he slammed his window shut.

I looked down to see Dowe smirking at me.

I turned my attention back to Phil. "We have less than 18 hours. Better get back to our cells before we arouse suspicion for being up here."

I left without saying goodbye to any of them. My brain was already occupied with working out a schematic for tampering with the machines, and I didn't have the energy to waste on civility.

John and Dowe crowed bedtime wishes that I ignored. Phil said nothing, but I knew she was watching me again.

16

I was up all night working on a plan to force the factory to self-destruct.

Designing a schematic to overload the machines wasn't particularly difficult. I could think of a couple of ways to redirect the chemicals, the easiest one being to drain everything into the holding vats.

What stretched the limits of my college education was figuring out a way to explain that plan to Phil. For our sabotage to work, I would need her to monitor the gauges on the side of the storage tanks and reroute the flow when I told her to. It wasn't difficult, but if she flipped the wrong switch, we might flood the entire island with gaseous Red Rain.

Meanwhile, I would need to hack into the office computer, override the factory's automatic functions, and crack the firewall so I could upload the virus to a server on the mainland.

All of this needed to be done in about twenty minutes, or however long John and Dowe could keep Ambrose distracted. And I wasn't exactly the world's most competent hacker.

I scarfed down breakfast and then took the scenic route back to my cell, passing under Tower's lookout.

"Your lockdown starts in 2 minutes, 120518," he called down by way of warning.

I glanced at the mix of guards and prisoners milling about. "Yeah, and I'm bored. Got any coloring supplies?"

There was a pause, then a permanent marker hit me on the head. I stooped to pick it up. "Any paper?"

He snorted. "Why do you think I was using my arm to track your laps?"

I wasn't about to acknowledge that. I pocketed the marker and hurried back to my cell.

The deadbolt clicked shut right on schedule—8 AM, end of breakfast hour. I looked around the room for anything I could both write on and transport. The sheets would work, but that seemed excessive. I rooted under the bed and found my dirty shirt from yesterday.

I spread it out on the floor. Marker in hand, I closed my eyes and recalled a snapshot of the controls on the holding tanks. I waited until the image crystalized, and then I started sketching.

I was almost done when I became aware of an increase in the ambient noise. It was hard to quantify through the concrete walls of my cell, but there was definitely agitated activity going on in the yard. I scribbled faster.

Something that sounded like an explosion—or fireworks— went off. And then a heavy bass beat kicked in.

I hesitated, for a brief minute regretting that I'd left the important task of "distraction" to John and Dowe.

At that moment, the lock on my door clicked open.

Balling the shirt under my arm, I checked to make sure I had the drive in my pocket. I cracked open the door to my cell and looked around.

Mercifully, there were no guards. However, half of my floor mates were also standing in the now-open doorways of their own cells.

I guess it looked less suspicious if an entire wing went offline.

Several of the older and wiser ones gazed at me, as if subconsciously understanding that I was likely to blame.

"Wow!" I said with a glee that did not match my age. "Sounds like a party out there. Glad we've got the day off!"

That did the trick. A cheer went up. More cells opened as people called to their companions, and a consensus of inmates flowed to the stairs. I blended seamlessly with the crowd and followed them out to the yard.

As soon as the doors burst open, we were assaulted with hideous pop music. The song was at least fifty years old, which meant it was uncensored—a clever touch. Why they couldn't have gone a few more decades back and picked something worth listening to, I don't know, but beggars can't be choosers.

The atmosphere in the yard was more like a party than a riot. I couldn't see what was going on through the crowd, but some stray balloons were floating away into the sky, and I heard fireworks going off. The air also smelled sickeningly sweet. I couldn't put my finger on the taste, but when I heard a chant for "more sprinkles" rippling through the crowd, I decided I'd better not ask.

Whatever they were doing, it was working. Guards were flowing from all corners of the island, and I heard a siren from one of the towers. It synced surprisingly well with the pop music.

I slinked along the barracks until I was close enough to dart into the shadows of the factory. I waited around the corner and watched the door for one minute, two.

More guards scurried towards the commotion. A second siren joined the chase. And then, finally, Ambrose emerged from the factory.

He took one look at the mess in the yard and groaned. Muttering under his breath, he stormed towards the crowd, cocking his gun.

I slipped into the building. The guards at the first and second doors had already vacated their posts. The secretary at the elevator, however, had not.

She looked at me over her nose. I collected myself. "I'm late for work."

She groaned and paged me in. "Don't make me do this again," she said, as if pressing the button with her manicured fingernails required all the energy she had to give for the day. "Or I'll report you."

"Go right on ahead," I muttered as I stepped into the elevator.

Phil rushed to meet me as soon as the doors opened. I shoved the shirt into her hands.

"This is a diagram of the control panels on the side of the holding tanks. If you flip these switches, it will drain all the product from the factory into the two main holding tanks and seal them off." I heaved, realizing with chagrin that I was out of breath.

Phil squinted at my scribbles. I pointed as I talked. "If you move these dials to the right numbers, it will begin to chill the gas to the point of condensing. Then all we have to do is puncture the bottom of the holding tanks, and the liquid acid will drain safely out the bottom."

"Safe" was a relative term, of course.

Phil glanced across the factory, mentally calibrating the plan. "Got it."

"Wait until I give the signal. I have to shut down production first, and then the tanks have to fill completely before we can close them off and condense the gas. Don't touch anything until I tell you to."

I hoped the emphasis in my voice was enough to make my point. I didn't wait to find out. I jogged into the office; Phil had wisely left the door open for me.

I was greeted by the thrum of an ancient printer as it obliviously continued to spit out paper. I looked at the stack that was rapidly building up on the tray and shook my head. Ambrose always had been a waste of resources.

I tapped the screen in the center of the desk, and a trio of monitors glowed to life. A beautiful array of control programs was running. The biggest one, displayed on the center monitor, tracked the progress of the weapon being pumped into a special transport container on the surface. Ambrose had wisely paused this delicate process before he left the room.

They'd made the economical but daring choice to transport the weapon in liquid form, which made my job much simpler. All I had to do was reroute it back into the factory and then empty the holding vat. Because all the pipes and hoses were still connected, it took only a few clicks on the control panel to reverse the flow and drain the product back into one of the holding tanks. It was easy—too easy—and I could only hope that wasn't a premonition.

The printer hesitated in the middle of a page. With an angry chirp, it spit the rest of the paper out blank and started printing a different report.

While the acid drained back into the factory, I swiped through the other applications. The hard part would be dealing with the Red Rain that was still flowing through the factory. The weapon was produced in gaseous form, which meant I had to halt production, collect the product in the second holding tank, and condense it—a multistep process the system wasn't designed for.

That said, the software wasn't too complex—after all, they expected Ambrose to monitor it—so I quickly found the control panel that let me halt production.

I tapped on it, and it informed me that the login had timed out.

"Are you kidding me?" I yelled, in the most colorful way possible.

I had two login options. I could use face recognition, but there was no way I'd fool the camera into thinking I was Ambrose, not with my mustache and overall good looks. The other option was a passcode. I could try to hack it, but we didn't have time.

I scanned the other applications, wondering if there was a redundancy I could exploit. Red text in the corner of one screen caught my eye: EMERGENCY SHUT DOWN.

I hit it, and it asked me to confirm—no security clearance needed.

I could shut the entire factory down, but there was no telling what kind of alarms would go off when I did. I might only have minutes before Ambrose came rushing back, and in the meantime, I'd have to chill the remaining product manually. Emergency mode would no doubt lock Phil out of the control panel on the tanks.

It could be done—I knew where the right levers were—but I'd have to do it. There was no way I could explain it to Phil.

I closed my eyes and ran the numbers. I would need to find a place to upload the virus and have it ready to launch. I would wait until the product on the surface had finished draining. Then I would have Phil reroute the pipes so that the product in the factory would begin to flow into the tanks. I would engage the emergency shut-off and immediately upload the virus, before running to chill the product and drain both tanks. That way, if someone showed up before I got back to the office, the damage would already be done.

It could be done. But only if I could find a decent place to upload this virus.

I toggled through the open programs. Ambrose's email was logged in, but that wasn't good enough; even the government wouldn't be stupid enough to open a suspicious attachment from Ambrose.

I opened a browser. Uploading to a very public website might work—except I quickly found that Ambrose's computer wasn't connected to the internet. I tried several URLs, and everything was blocked. A glance at the toolbar showed that the computer was connected to something, but it was apparently a private internal network.

I cursed. I knew beyond a shadow of a doubt that wiping this terminal alone wouldn't be enough. It might set them back a few months, but it wouldn't erase the data. I needed to wipe all of their servers, or at least most of them. That should take care of Red Rain, as well as give them several more pressing problems to worry about. Even Smyrna wouldn't be able to reconstruct their empire after I wiped them clean.

I tugged on my mustache, a habit I thought I'd abandoned in college. It made no sense for Ambrose's computer to be totally offline. Not only was it out of character for the government—they liked everything to be connected at all times so they could monitor it from anywhere—but they had to be tracking the progress in the factory somehow. There's no way they were *actually* making Ambrose fax paper reports.

A glance at the other screen revealed that the shipping container was almost empty. At least five minutes had passed—I needed to figure this out, and *now*.

I opened the control panel and rapidly clicked through all available submenus. Even if this computer was only linked to an internal network, surely someone else had access to that network. Was there a shared folder or database?

Jackpot. My panicked digging was rewarded—Ambrose had access to several shared databases. I opened them all, scanning the folders to find the one with the most traffic.

The printer screeched, exactly at the right moment to cover the oath that left my lips.

These weren't just any databases. These were high-profile government databases, and the United was clearly planning a war.

Everything from Project 74 was there—all the weapons I had ever designed were in production. They'd also created dozens of other ballistics—everything from nuclear warheads to mines big enough to turn an entire city into a crater. There was even interstellar weaponry; whatever war they were planning, they weren't afraid to take it to the skies.

And, of course, there was an entire database on Red Rain.

A respectful terror seized my soul, but it also sent my gears spinning. This armory could win any war. What you didn't bomb you could melt with Red Rain. If the United got all these weapons into production, there would be nothing stopping them.

And right now, there was nothing stopping me from copying them all to the flash drive.

The printer continued to yell. I glanced at it and saw that it was out of paper. *I do not have time to deal with this!* I hit the button to turn off the wireless connection, and the device silenced.

Turning back to the computer, I pulled the drive out of my pocket. How much storage was on here? I looked around and mercifully found a port on the side of the monitor. Opening up the drive, I started copying the entire Red Rain database and a prime selection of the other folders, as much as I could fit.

While the drive synced, I checked the status and saw that the shipping container had fully drained back into the factory. I had to act fast if I wanted to make it out of here alive; a pocketful of war wouldn't do me any good if Ambrose caught me in his office and murdered me on the spot.

I leaned my head out the door. "Now, Phil!"

I saw her grab a dial and crank with vehemence. I hoped it was the right one, but honestly, I wasn't worried about the factory anymore. It would give me great joy to destroy it, but even if the United had a tankful of Red Rain, they couldn't stop me once I had all of these other delightful weapons.

I went back to the drive and found the virus. I copied it into the main folder of the most prominent-looking database, then removed the drive from the computer. I tabbed back to the emergency override panel.

Twisting the drive in my fingers, I rehearsed the steps in my head. Shut down the factory, launch the virus, drain the tanks—if I could—and then get out of here before Ambrose came. Did I even care about the tanks? If I could get away with this drive, I'd have everything I needed to cut myself off from the United. And if Ambrose didn't find me here, he'd probably blame Phil for the sabotage. It would at least buy me enough time to hide the drive somewhere I could retrieve it later.

I took a deep breath. There was no guarantee I could get off this island alive. But if I could…

It would have been worth it.

I hit the button and sent the factory into emergency shut down.

17

Instantly, the display exploded in a firework of warnings and flashing buttons. The control panels locked as a dozen popups prompted me to confirm or override the state of emergency. They all required a passcode, so there was nothing I could do but let the automatic program run its course.

I heard the factory change gears, and lights all across the cavern switched from green to red or orange. But, pleasantly, I didn't hear any sirens. I was sure anyone monitoring the factory remotely would see a warning, but hopefully they were all too far away—or too busy observing the spectacle of John and Dowe—to respond immediately.

It looked like Phil had correctly rerouted the flow, and the last of the weapon was beginning to fill the holding tank. I tabbed back to the file directory and found the virus. Setting the drive down on the desk so I could use both hands, I opened the computer's command window and typed the magic words.

I might not know how to code viruses, but I was an expert at launching them.

I felt satisfaction mold my lips into something like a smile. There was no telling how far the virus would spread. The government did love a secure database; the virus might just take a lap around whatever office Ambrose was synced to and then go no further. But even if that's all it did, it was going to create one beautiful mess. Their secret armory was about to go up in digital smoke, and I could only hope some fat, lazy politicians were sitting at their desks right now to witness it.

I closed my eyes, breathed in the moment, and hit enter.

At first, nothing happened, which was what I expected. I clicked on a random item and was greeted with an error about the file being "unavailable." I refreshed the folder, and the file list went blank.

I clicked on another folder and found the same thing. I backed out several levels, each time revealing a deeper and deeper vacuum of empty space. Soon the entire database was gone.

I rewarded myself with a cackle. "Ephesus, you dirty little genius."

I clicked on another database, but the file explorer froze. I tried going in another way and only got an angry screech.

Flashing alerted me out of my peripheral. I turned to the other monitor to see one of the control programs glitching out like it had been possessed.

Two more windows followed suit. Soon the whole display was throbbing with errors and pixelated graphics like the entire computer was being choked to death.

I jumped when Phil screamed. I ran to the window and heard rather than saw the commotion. The factory hadn't shut down—if anything, it was working harder than before. Every machine was churning at full speed while every display flickered in a panic. Raw chemicals rushed into the factory to fulfill the imaginary quota—but they had nowhere to go. The pipes we had sealed off swelled, bloated like beached whales.

I saw it coming with only enough time to mutter an appropriate oath. The pipes burst, releasing my invisible angel of death into the air.

So much for not flooding the island with Red Rain.

I raced back to the computer and tried a program, any program, but the terminal was unresponsive. The entire screen was locked up, the corrupted applications twitching in their death throes.

The virus was consuming programs as well as data files. Whether that was by design or poor programming, I'll never know.

I wasn't entirely surprised by this turn of events, but the computer didn't know what to do with itself. The only thing it could process was that factory was in a state of emergency, and it responded appropriately.

I recognized what was happening with only seconds to spare. I raced out of the office, waving my arms to get her attention.

"Phil, get out of there!" I yelled at the top of my lungs, hoping she could hear me over the din. "The entire system is failing!"

She stood up, face pinched in confusion. Why she wasn't already running was beyond me. I tried to make myself clear with wild hand gestures. "You need to get out of there! The computer thinks the factory is on fire and it's going to—"

I needn't have bothered. The sirens and pulsing lights that ignited just then made the situation clear. The emergency sprinklers engaged, and my weapon made its debut.

Phil screamed, but she was upstaged by the symphonic hiss as the spraying water married the gases in the air and condensed into liquid fire. Red Rain showered over the factory, the drops of acid sparkling like cursed rubies, bathing the room in corrosion and death.

I took a defensive step back, but I appeared to be safe. The office and the path to the elevator were, wisely, on a different fire suppression system.

Phil was not so lucky. The alcove was sheltered enough, but the rest of the factory was covered in the downpour. The walkway leading to the holding tanks was slick and glistening, and it was only a matter of minutes before the acid ate the metal and trapped her for good.

If we could find something to cover her head, she might be able to make it before the pathway washed out. She'd get a few burns, but that would be better than dying, I assumed.

I started shouting at her to that effect, but she interrupted me. "The emergency panel by the door! Shut off the sprinklers!"

I glanced in the direction she was pointing. There was an emergency access panel in the far corner by the elevator—the elevator Ambrose would no doubt come storming out of any minute.

I abruptly remembered the drive sitting on the desk. I had to get the drive and put it somewhere Ambrose wouldn't find it. It was my only chance at freedom—and even if I couldn't get out of this alive, I definitely didn't want the United to have my copy of Red Rain *or* Ephesus's mastermind virus.

"Just hang on!" I yelled. "I need to grab the drive! Don't move!"

I darted back into the office and snatched the drive off the desk. Clenching it in my fist, I paused in the middle of the floor and weighed my options. Hiding the drive in the factory seemed unwise—I might not have access to the factory after today, if it didn't burn itself to the ground. I could hide it on my person, but I knew that, no matter how much blame I tried to bestow on Phil, Ambrose would correctly assume I had been the primary instigator. I would be receiving the brunt of the interrogation and any invasive searches.

It dawned on me that Phil was actually the safest place to store the drive. Ambrose would never assume she was carrying weapons, and at the very least, he would be too preoccupied to search her immediately.

Yes, giving the drive back to Phil was my best bet—which meant I definitely needed to get her out of here alive.

I looked out the office window in her direction—and stopped.

Despite devoting my entire adult life to the project, I had never seen my weapon in action, but now the effects of it were on full display. The entire factory was coated in blood, the emergency lights reflecting off every acid-wet surface. The factory seemed to be melting away as Red Rain chewed at the metal, stripping the finish from the machines and gnawing holes in the pipework. The smell of corroding iron and steel choked the air, even in the office.

It worked. My weapon really, truly worked, and it did everything it was supposed to. It *was* the perfect weapon. Released during a rainstorm, Red Rain could burn an entire city to the ground, and there would be no kill switch to stop it.

I glanced at the holding tanks and imagined how many cities—countries—the United could have melted with the contents. I knew exactly what the United would do with the weapon: They would rain it on every errant country that had refused to join their conglomerate. Every last holdout of individuality would be brought to its knees or burned to the ground.

And if anyone dared rebel, the United could simply wash them off the map. Primitive countries, the poor, stubborn religions—anything they didn't want or need could be scalded to death, until the entire planet was conformed to their idiosyncratic mold.

That was, of course, if I didn't shoot first.

Phil's shrieking shattered my thoughts. I turned towards the holding tanks, but she was no longer there. Had she made a run for it?

I scanned the factory, and my fears were confirmed—Red Rain had destroyed the walkway to the alcove. Several chunks were missing from the middle. Phil was nowhere to be seen.

My brain skipped a beat. Had she—? I pressed my face to the office window, searching the factory floor for her body, but saw nothing.

The flash of moving metal caught the corner of my eye. I looked up to see Phil dangling from a broken catwalk, suspended several stories in the air.

I watched in horrified admiration as she hauled herself back onto what was left of the platform. I retraced her path; she'd been smart enough to find another way out of the alcove. She'd climbed up the side of the tanks and onto a service catwalk that hung below the ceiling. She was out of range of the sprinklers but not out of harm's way; Red Rain had eaten away at the chains supporting the catwalk, and she'd nearly plunged to her death.

As it was, she'd only postponed the inevitable.

And so have you.

I looked down at the drive in my hand. If the United didn't start a war with Red Rain, I would. If Smyrna couldn't reconstruct the formula for them, they'd come after me for it. We'd chase each other in circles until one of us pulled the trigger, and then this is how humanity would end: The last holdout clinging to life while Red Rain set the world on fire.

It was just a matter of who made the first move. If it mattered at all.

You're the only one who can end this, Nic.

I scanned the office. The desktop was useless—but my eyes fell on the printer. I had taken it offline, which meant it was safe from the virus and presumably still operational.

I found the port and jammed the drive in. The screen brightened with a chirp, and the file list loaded.

The printer bemoaned its lack of paper. I tuned it out as I began to manually delete every file that didn't belong to Ephesus. It was agonizingly tedious, and the decades-old electronic ran at a snail's pace.

Clattering metal from outside the office reminded me that I needed to hurry. I wiped all the weapons files I had copied from the United's database, and then I came to Red Rain.

I stared at it, a million computations firing in my mind. Then, with a curse and a sigh, I deleted it.

18

I yanked the drive out. I assumed the printer didn't have any kind of file recovery, but for good measure I hit the button to bring the device back online.

Pocketing the drive, I raced out of the office and looked for Phil. She lay completely still on the swaying platform high above. Red Rain gushed from the broken sprinkler pipes right beneath her.

The sprinklers! I turned towards the elevator. There was a dry path to the emergency panel, the spray of the sprinklers falling just short of the wall. I could make it—but probably only because I was lanky and agile.

I flattened myself against the wall and started sliding towards the door. "Philadelphia!" I shouted to get her attention.

There was a beat, and I wondered if she hadn't heard me. Then a weak "You idiot!" came floating down.

You can do better than that, but okay. "I'm coming!"

"Ten minutes too late!"

Fair.

I made it to the panel. A swift fist shattered the protective glass, and I began rapidly flipping all the levers off, ignoring the blood that formed on my knuckles. I took the sprinklers offline, followed by the equipment and, for good measure, most of the power.

The sirens ceased as the entire factory ground to a halt. The headache-inducing whir died away, and the lights on the machines went dark. The room shuddered and sighed, as if glad to be put out of its misery.

Most importantly, the sprinklers turned off. I turned around and watched the water dry up, taking the hiss of Red Rain with it. Soon the room was shockingly silent.

I walked up to the edge of the platform, avoiding the standing puddles. I scanned what was left of the walkway and judged it to be useless. It was only a matter of time before the rest of the weakened metal snapped, and it didn't go out nearly far enough to catch Phil if she fell.

I leaned over and looked at the factory floor below. It was a deadly mess of broken pipes, scraps of metal, and pools of Red Rain. But those puddles were slowly shrinking as they ate through the concrete floor and bled into the earth below.

Eventually, the floor would be passable—but how long would that take?

"Just hang on!" I yelled up at her. "As soon as a path clears, we'll get you down!"

I scanned the factory for anything helpful—a ladder, a lift, rope—but saw nothing. After a beat, I realized Phil hadn't responded. I looked up at her. "Did you hear me, Phil?"

"I don't think we have time to wait!" The fear turned her voice into a warble. "These chains aren't going to hold!"

She pointed. Even from this distance I could see that Red Rain had weakened most of the chains supporting the catwalk. It was only a matter of time—maybe minutes—before more of them snapped and sent her plummeting to her death.

An angry yell disrupted my mental attempt to solve that problem. "What have you done?"

I turned to see Ambrose standing in the elevator, gawking at our handiwork. I groaned. I did not have time to deal with him right now, but maybe if I could keep him engaged long enough to get Phil down, we could at least make it out of the factory before he murdered us all.

"What did you expect?" I cracked with a sarcasm that, for once in my life, I didn't feel. "You left *her* alone unsupervised."

It didn't work. He charged, and I didn't have enough time to brace myself. He slammed me backward into the railing, almost flipping me over into the factory below. The corroded fence groaned and shifted but held.

I stood up—right into a punch to the face.

Colors swam before my eyes. I could barely see, but I managed to avoid the next hit. I was attempting to focus on his hands through my blurred vision and didn't see the kick until it was too late.

Pain ricocheted through my body. I involuntarily buckled over and backed up, trying to give myself space to find a better defensive position.

Ambrose gave me no such luxury. He charged at me. I sidestepped to avoid him—right onto what was left of the walkway.

I realized my mistake a moment too late. Ambrose blocked the way and continued his approach, slow and menacing this time. I stood up to meet him, even though my body was still screaming from the kick.

"I hope you enjoyed your little act of rebellion." He took another step. I backed down the walkway, feeling it creak and shudder beneath me.

"Because once you're out of the picture, we'll just rebuild and pick up right where we left off."

He jabbed my shoulder, hard. I coughed. I glanced behind me and realized there were only a few paces left between me and my doom—if I was going to enjoy my victory, I had to do it now.

I met Ambrose's eyes. "I know you will—after you finish repairing all the damage from the virus I just released onto your perfect little United internet."

He glared at me in confusion. I straightened until I towered over him. This time, the sarcasm in my voice was proud and genuine. "You really do have great upload speed, especially for being so far out in the ocean."

I'm sure he didn't fully understand what I meant, but he knew I'd done him dirty, and it infuriated him. I soaked in his anger—my last mistake. I wasn't prepared to dodge the backhanded slap he landed on my face.

I stumbled backward to the end of the walkway. Ambrose closed the gap. I scanned the shredded factory floor beneath me, trying to spy a safe place to make the jump.

I registered Phil screeching at Ambrose, begging him to spare me. He paused to cast threats in her direction—just long enough for me to predict his next move.

He lunged at me. I ducked, and his cumbersome form stumbled over me. I swung at his legs, sending him over the edge.

He landed face-first in a puddle of Red Rain with a smack and several other unpleasant sounds.

Before I could even draw a breath, Phil screamed again, this time in tune with a snapping chain. I looked up to see her scrambling at the pathway as it bucked under the strain.

"Nic!" she gasped.

The other chain broke, at the same time something in me cracked.

She fell backward into the factory below, her dark hair fanning around her like a funeral shroud. I could come up with no sound, no words, no heroic ideas—just one burst of a very cold, very heavy, and very unfamiliar emotion.

Regret.

Then I judged her trajectory, and the world restarted. She crashed to the ground—right on top of Ambrose, whose voluminous frame absorbed the brunt of her fall. She flailed like a ragdoll, and then her head fell back and cracked onto the concrete. She went limp without a sound.

I spied a piece of fallen walkway that formed a temporary island of safety. I jumped onto it, then, in the most twisted game of "the floor is lava," navigated to Phil's side. The ends of her hair grazed a puddle of acid as I lifted her. I laid her out on the piece of fallen walkway like a stretcher.

I felt her neck. Her pulse was weak but steady, her breathing even. Her leg was burned in several places, but it was superficial. She'd probably get a nice scar out of the deal, but she would recover.

I sat down on the metal next to her to wait. I was sure the rest of the guards would come running soon enough to fish us out.

I glanced at Ambrose. It looked like Red Rain would spare them the expense of a burial.

I looked around the still factory. The last drops of my weapon dripped silently from the ruined machinery. The tired fluorescents high above reflected off the pools of blood. I watched as the puddle nearest to me gurgled through the concrete and wondered, dryly, if this was the last I'd ever see of my creation.

Into the silence, I laughed.

EPILOGUE: TOWER

I drummed my fingers on my tablet and waited for John and Dowe to decide how many crimes they wanted to be responsible for.

"I didn't do anything! I'm innocent!"

"Now, John, we talked about this. The whole point of staging a distraction is to take responsibility away from someone else." Dowe spelled the situation out with his hands, at least as best he could with both wrists cuffed to the chair. "If we confess to organizing an impromptu British baking contest on the lawn, then they won't blame Phil for blowing up the factory."

That wasn't how any of this worked—if for no other reason than you couldn't have a "British" bakeoff on an American prison island—but I wasn't about to tell them that. I had no desire to make this debate any longer than it already was.

John crooned as what few neurons he had fired in understanding. "Ohh, right. Then I did it—I did *all* of it! I stole the flour from the cafeteria, I borrowed Captain Stricklin's hairpins to use as toothpicks, I dogeared Cloud's book to save my place…"

"Wait, that was *you*? You monster."

"Gentlemen, focus, please," I inserted, even though I knew I'd get more compliance from a roomful of cats. "I need to turn in this report."

Dowe shrugged. "Just send them the pictures of the grand prize winner—that will tell them everything they need to know."

I scrolled through the evidence on the tablet's camera roll. "Yes, I'm sure pictures of a cake that looks vaguely like the gates of Mordor will explain everything."

"Listen, Attila did the best he could with forty-five minutes and margarine instead of butter. He is a visionary." John leaned forward, nostrils flaring as if he was prepared to go to war for this guy's baking skills.

"His genius will be lost on the higher-ups. *Lord of the Rings* has been censored for thirty years—I'm sure none of them have read it." I groaned and tossed the tablet on the desk. I'm not sure why I was trying so hard; there was nothing I could put in this report that would make it any easier on them. The situation was clear: John and Dowe had staged a riot to cover another inmate's act of terrorism. The fact that the riot involved frosting instead of weapons would not lighten their punishment.

What's worse, it was only a matter of time before my superiors figured out that I had been involved, and it was my turn to be cuffed to a chair.

"Did it work?"

I looked up to see Dowe staring at me, eyes disturbingly lucid. "Did they succeed?"

I glanced out the window, where crews swarmed in a panic around the ruined weapons factory in the middle of the yard. "Yes," I said, finally pausing to take a breath and appreciate that fact. "They did."

"Then write whatever you want in the report." Dowe gestured with his shoulder at my abandoned tablet. "It doesn't matter. It was worth it."

I thanked him with a smile.

Just then, John's phone rang.

We all froze while we appreciated the nuance of that revelation. Not only did John have a phone—something he definitely wasn't supposed to have—but it was working. Nic's virus had rendered most of the electronics on the island useless; I'd had to scrounge in a storage closet for an outdated tablet just to write my report.

Both Dowe and I stared at John as his pocket continued to trill. He squirmed. "Could, uh, someone get that for me? I don't think I can reach…" He tried to contort himself around his cuffs.

"I'll get it, I'll get it…" I got up and gingerly reached into the pocket of John's jumpsuit, ignoring the other pieces of contraband he had crammed in there. I pulled out an ancient flip phone. The case was so scratched that the original color was ambiguous, and it nearly fell apart at seam when I opened it.

The pixelated screen obscured most of the caller's number. All I could make out was the country code: 234.

I answered the call and put it on speaker. "Hello?"

A woman's voice pierced the crackly connection. "You're not Dowe *or* John," she accused, her words thickened by the ghost of an African dialect.

"Thankfully," I deadpanned. "Who are you?"

"Their boss."

I arched my eyebrows and looked to John and Dowe for confirmation.

John huffed and rocked his chair. "I answer to no one!"

Dowe handled the situation with much more diplomacy. "Jael!" he crooned. "I thought you'd forgotten about us."

"Honey, the only one doing any forgetting in this operation is you," she returned, but not unkindly.

Even Dowe couldn't deny that.

"Operation?" I prodded. I knew John and Dowe were rebels, and they had some connections. I just never expected those connections to amount to anything.

"Sugar, no offense," the woman replied in a tone loaded with offense, "but that information is classified."

"Good, I didn't want to be involved in any more schemes today anyway," I muttered. "Would you like to talk to John instead?"

"No, I want to talk to Dowe."

"Yes! I knew I was the favorite!" he crowed.

Her sigh rattled the dying speaker. "You're not the favorite. You're just the first."

First of what? I thought but dared not ask. I took the phone off speaker and balanced it on Dowe's shoulder.

"Yeah huh, Dowe here. Yeah, don't worry, I'm having him move to the *other* side of the desk."

Dowe glared and gestured roughly at me. I put my hands up and backed away.

"Okay, go ahead." Muffled chatter came through the line as Dowe continued to carry on his conversation. John leaned over as far as he could without tipping the chair over, struggling to hear.

"Uh huh. Yup, threat neutralized. Yeah, virus was Q's doing. Oh, you saw that? Man, can you send me the link? Oh I know, isn't she the greatest?"

She? Does he mean Philadelphia? My blood chilled when I remembered that not everyone on this island was expendable.

"Yeah, she'll be okay. A little bonked up but no worse than me. Oh, that's a great idea! See, this is why you're the big boss lady." Dowe turned a toothy grin on John, who copied the gesture—even though he clearly had no idea what was going on, even more so than usual.

"Yeah, I'll send her right over. You should bring Q too. Yeah, I know he's annoying and antisocial," Dowe punctuated the statement with an eyeroll, "but if you give him a chance, I think he'll prove useful."

"Debatable," John muttered, and I would have laughed if the whole exchange weren't vaguely threatening.

The woman on the other end asked a sharp question. "Who, him?" Dowe answered. "Yeah, Tower's cool. I'm sure he can help." He looked up at me, face scrunched in a question mark.

I returned it with a glare. "What are you signing me up for?"

Dowe winked. "He said yes. Okay, we're on it. Hey, have you thought about my offer to take you out to dinner? Wow, no answer? Rude but okay…"

He nodded at me. I walked over and snatched the phone.

"Welcome, newest recruit," the woman chirped as soon as I put the speaker to my ear.

"I didn't agree to anything," I said, mostly just for posterity.

"Didn't ask."

This woman clearly had the same impeccable logic as John and Dowe. "Then how do you know you can trust me?"

"It will get your niece to safety."

I slapped my hand over the phone and glanced at John and Dowe, but they were whispering and giggling conspiratorially amongst themselves and weren't paying attention. I stepped a few feet away and turned my back to them, lowering my voice. "How did you…"

"That's what I thought. Listen, sugar, all you need to know is that I've got a plan and the resources to back up that plan. Here's what you're going to do." She continued to rattle off instructions without giving me a breath to argue. "I'm sending you 'orders' to have Philadelphia and the doctor deported to the mainland for questioning. You're going to put them on a helicopter and fly them to the waypoint I give you, where my associates will put them on a train. That train is going to get 'hijacked,' and I'll take it from there. Understood?"

It wasn't the plan I was struggling to understand. I reached inside my army jacket and fingered my rosary, weighing the odds of survival. Philadelphia didn't have many other options. If she stayed here, the government would execute her for destroying their factory. I had connections, but none that could get her off the island. Trusting her to a stranger—especially one that worked with John and Dowe—was a game of Russian roulette, but I'd rather take a bet than hand her over to a firing squad.

I took a deep breath and gave the woman one last chance to buy my trust. "And what will you do with her when she arrives?"

Her laugh crackled the line. "We're going to save the world."

TO BE CONTINUED...

WANT EXCLUSIVE BONUS SCENES?

Become a Patron and get access to **exclusive bonus scenes** for this series! This bonus content is not available anywhere else, and I post a new scene every month. Plus, you can get digital ARCs, signed paperbacks, collector's edition hardbacks, and merch, or read my WIP as I write it!

Become a Patron at:
patreon.com/rachelnewhouse

Or sign up for my newsletter and be the first to hear about new releases—plus get sneak peeks of upcoming books, cover art, and more!

Sign up at:
rachelnewhouse.com/subscribe

DID YOU LOVE THIS BOOK?

Please consider leaving a review on Amazon or Goodreads! It's one of the most important things you can do to support an indie author. Thank you!

HI FROM RACHEL

Rachel Newhouse is an author, wife, secretary, and Sunday school teacher from Kansas City, Missouri. Her obsessions are sci-fi, dystopian, and kid lit. When she's not writing, she's cooking Asian food, growing chilis that are too spicy to eat, and watching wildly age-inappropriate shows like *My Little Pony* and *Gravity Falls* with her husband, Joe. She also really likes glitter. You've been warned.

Connect with Rachel:
bio.site/rachelnewhouse

DAVID ALSO SAYS HI

David Hartung is "that guy"—the one whose fanfic became canon. If you're jealous of that, you're right to be. Outside of that claim to fame, he lives in Wisconsin with his family, where his firstborn Daniel continually robs him of his aspirations to become a master of the secret art of Narco.

www.ingramcontent.com/pod-product-compliance
Lightning Source LLC
Chambersburg PA
CBHW070514200726
48293CB00007B/2528